BLOSSOMS *in the* GRAVEYARD

Birendra Kumar Bhattacharyya

Translated from original Assamese *Kabor Aru Phool*
by MITRA PHUKAN

NIYOGI
BOOKS

Published by
NIYOGI BOOKS
D-78, Okhla Industrial Area, Phase-I
New Delhi-110 020, INDIA
Tel: 91-11-26816301, 49327000
Fax: 91-11-26810483, 26813830
email: niyogibooks@gmail.com
website: www.niyogibooksindia.com

Layout Design: Ganga Kumar
Cover Design: Misha Oberoi

ISBN: 978-93-85285-47-9

Publication: 2016

Printed at: Niyogi Offset Pvt. Ltd., New Delhi, India

Dedicated to those men, women and children who sacrificed all that they held precious in the course of the Bangladesh War of Liberation

&

To the many readers and admirers of Jnanpith Awardee
Dr Birendra Kumar Bhattacharyya's works

*

For Rupam and Rittique
...so that the future can learn from the past

1

We did not take the good road. The one that we did take had been planned and constructed at least half a century ago during the British era. It was an uneven, winding track. There were numerous bends as well. For tired travellers, there was only the open-armed invitation of the soft damp red earth along the roadside to minimize the discomfort of the sight of the rough track. Sometimes, the Hajong farmers would look at us with simple curiosity, a reminder of the racist sufferings being inflicted on the East Pakistanis. The higher we climbed, the more we saw dense forests huddled together in the cold, like an unknown country.

Even though we had travelled at least forty miles, we had not met a single person from the Garo tribe. Our Jeep had been whining in different pitches. Sometimes, it screeched whimsically like a small boy when we tried to take it out from the mudhole. At other times, it sang happily in its own rough voice on getting a good stretch of road. A gust of wind slanted in with a shower of rain to whisper damply in my ear, 'Not here - your destination is higher up.'

'Why did you bring us by this road?' Bagaitkar asked. 'There must be another way. If this is the main road, then I am Mahatma Gandhi!'

The often-taken path just had too many potholes, hence I chose the lesser-known path.

He laughed. The beads of rain that glistened on his curly hair looked like drops of sacred water sprinkled on his head. From his eyes, something seemed to tremble like the beams radiating from the eyes of a golden cat. When he turned to look at me, it seemed as though he was at peace, but the searing sadness of his mind was apparent in the lines on his face.

I was remorseful. I had heard, a long time ago, that a new road was being built from Krishnai to Tura. I was under the impression that the road was shorter, though unsurfaced. True to character, I had decided to ignore that road and come on this old one from Lakhipur. Compared to Bagaitkar, I was less courageous and daring when it came to leaving a known path and taking an unknown one. Could I keep up with him?

However, I had no idea that this road was in such a poor condition. I had not come this way for the last three years. I could not understand why this road had deteriorated so much during this time. Bagaitkar, though, would think it meaningless to look for a reason for this. He placed great importance on reaching Tura quickly for he was scheduled to meet up with a couple of freedom fighters and leaders from Bangladesh. If we continued at this pace, there was no hope of reaching Tura before four. We had not even reached Phulbari yet.

Bagaitkar's irony was quite apparent in his comment. He insinuated through gestures and signs that I was wrong and had brought them through a path that was not the main road. Only if Bagaitkar morphed into Mahatma Gandhi himself would this path transform itself into the main road. On the other hand, I knew quite well that this was indeed the main road. Thus, there was no need for Bagaitkar to turn into Mahatma Gandhi. Even so, I could not assert confidently that this path actually was the main road. Was this lack of confidence and self-doubt a sign of modesty and humility or was it a character flaw?

I waited wordlessly for my opportunity. The condition of the road began to improve as soon as the Jeep slowly came to the outskirts of Phulbari, which glowed in the distance. This sight gave me some consolation.

I had had that same diffident mental makeup from my childhood. Age had caught up with me. I had brought the Jeep on the correct path but my mentality remained unchanged. I could not say confidently, 'This is the main road. This is indeed the correct road to our destination.' On the other hand, I could not say that the road was not the right one either. We had come by the correct road. And yet, I had this hesitation, this dilemma. What could be the reason for this? I had no patience. I could not accept any religion, any mantra, any truth as being exact, accurate. It was nothingness. Only nothingness.

Bagaitkar was a karma yogi, a person who believed in the value of action. Once he deemed an action to be appropriate, he would wholeheartedly pursue its course. While moving ahead, he was never assailed by self-doubt on the way. Indeed, this was true even in the matter of bringing in change. For quite some time now, he had dedicated himself to the freedom struggles of different people and also to the struggles of poor workers and cultivators. He had travelled far and wide in the pursuit of this goal. He had been jailed for taking part in at least a hundred Satyagrahas. Let alone the pre-Independence era, even after Independence, Bagaitkar had worked and sacrificed, in however small a way, to free Hyderabad from the Razakars, Goa from the Portuguese, Arunachal from the Chinese and the people in general from undemocratic practices and soaring prices. He had not done all this for the sake of name, fame, fortune or power. He had been working for almost thirty years for the sake of satisfying his own conscience, for the sake of following the dictates of history, for the sake of the country.

He had come now to render help to the freedom struggle of Bangladesh. There was a relief organization, a Samiti, in Maharashtra. That relief organization had sent shoes, *lungis* (traditional male garment worn around the waist), medicines, mosquito nets, sleeveless cotton vests and other materials for the volunteers of the freedom struggle. He had brought them along with him. These were just a tiny fraction of the huge amount of materials that was required, a tiny peppercorn in a basket of huge kosu leaves. Not even a minute portion of the requirements of the volunteers would be met with this small quantity of material.

But Bagaitkar was an efficient person. He was eager to deliver even that peppercorn. Because it was only when peppercorns were added, one by one to the container, that the basket became full. Many people were critical, saying that the relief organization's money and materials did not reach the people, the real sufferers, who truly needed them. Some of the donated materials vanished midway. Many people in Gauhati and Tura, like those in other places, siphoned away much of the relief materials that were sent. There were all kinds of scandals about these misdemeanours. But Bagaitkar was unperturbed. There was no greed in his mind or in his behaviour. He had totally vanquished all covetousness through his power of discipline and self-control. He regularly carried out many tasks and did a lot of good work to control his mind despite not taking recourse to yoga, worship, rituals or religious chants.

Gradually, Phulbari came into view. The Jeep went forward through a soggy path. Even though the sun was out after the rain, it was not a fine, warm afternoon. The weather was gloomy. All around were rubbish dumps, shops and large crowds. A little way ahead was the hotel. As soon as I saw it, I remembered Pulin Babu. He was supposed to come here from Tangail.

The manager of the hotel was an old acquaintance. I had come to Tura several times before on different kinds of work. Once, I had come to stay with my brother. Tura is amazingly beautiful. It is the Shimla of India's North-East. The entry road was similar too. Though, unlike Himachal, there was no snowfall here, sometimes there would be frost. It would suddenly become damp and cold. A kind of clear grey light would pour down from the murky skies and the wind would sough past. While sitting at home and chatting within the family circle, a kind of domestic peace would settle on the mind.

In that small town, my nephew, my brother's son, met the Garo people. He had observed their beautiful world. He would sometimes sing a couple of Garo songs. Every now and then; he would ask me some random questions, which flustered me. We would all gorge on the food laid out for us. My sister-in-law's hospitality was flawless. I would sit and talk with my brother about governance in the hills.

It was always the same story. There was an agitation for self-governance in the Garo Hills going on at that time. That agitation resulted in the creation of the state of Meghalaya. There was not much that could be said, not much that could really be known. But it felt as though there was a fire burning within semi-clothed bodies. No doubt this fire was blazing, but it was scorching them as well. They had seen the shade and the glow of civilization. They were demanding roads, hospitals, schools, jobs, political power, trade and commerce. There was no bloodshed or violence even as they agitated for their demands. But even in that, the disease of civilization was evident. Nothing was in their hands. Trade and commerce was controlled by others. There was abundant land. But even in those lands, cultivators from East Pakistan had come and settled. Compared to the amount of yield that the immigrants' irrigated fields generated, the local jhum, the slash and burn agricultural practices, yielded very little. The towns that were established by means of these advanced agricultural practices and trade and commerce were all controlled by non-Garos. No doubt the ownership of the land was in the hands of the local Garos, but so what? Wealth and power were all in the hands of others.

I had come to the town in winter. I would walk towards the town centre every morning. It was a peaceful place. As in other towns, the court functioned there as well. It was governed by the Zila Council. But the monstrous rapacity had snatched all peace and beauty from the minds of the Garos. The real profits from trade in timber, cotton and fruits were all taken away by the outsiders.

The marketplace was heaving with the influx of both eatables and household articles from outside.

Walking around the town, I would come to a halt before Bhowmik's shop. Bhowmik was a much-needed man here. When the leaders of the Zila Council required something, Bhowmik, the shop owner, was summoned. Just like the mythical all-giving Kalpataru tree, he would manage, somehow or the other, to get it for them. The Garos, too, came to him to relax. Bhowmik spoke fluent Garo.

Sheal of Phulbari and Bhowmik of Tura—both were from East Bengal. They had come and settled here many years ago. An entire generation that had now passed away had spent their days here. The current generation was enjoying the fruits of their hard work. The kitchen of the hotel at Phulbari was like that of Annapurna, the goddess of food and abundance. Sheal would serve delicacies such as rohu and ari fish to the town's well-off people, getting fish from East Bengal to go with their rice. Even though the hotel was not too clean, travellers would not blame the uncleanliness, but would instead sympathize with Sheal and forgive him. To feed others was a virtuous and meritorious deed. It was not necessary to pay much attention to the manner of how one is fed. We, as a people, have endless strength when it comes to bearing up with injustice, dirt and inequality. For did life have any control over food and other worldly arrangements? This life was controlled by the deeds of the past life. The lifespan of a person was pre-ordained and set out on that person's horoscope.

Bhowmik would always greet me warmly and offer me a seat, as well as betel nuts and tea, even though it was not necessary. Gauging my mood, he would chat on topics that he judged I wished to talk about. He would create the impression that by going to his place, I had pleased and gratified not only him but also his family and relatives, and, indeed, the whole town.

Now, in Phulbari, Sheal exclaimed as soon as he saw me, 'Come, come, Robin Babu, it is my good fortune that I am meeting you like this. How is Munin Babu?' He was referring to my brother.

'Munin is in Shillong, Sheal Babu!' I gazed at Sheal with concern. I was amazed that the clear, youthful face that I had seen just the other day now reflected worry and negativity. 'Is something wrong? You've thinned down.'

Sheal Babu began to laugh. Putting his hand in his pocket, he slowly took out two cigarettes. He offered me one and took the other himself. Since I did not smoke, I did not take it. He lit up his own and said, 'What you see in my face is worry about money. Nothing else, really! There's nothing as bad as making money, you know, Robin Babu. I hear you write. Perhaps Saraswati, the goddess of learning, is not as cruel. Lakshmi must have been hurt during that churning of the ocean that took place between the gods and the asuras in mythic times.'

I smiled. 'Have you seen that owl that's named after the goddess of wealth? The Lakshmi owl?'

'Certainly I have. But I have seen this bird properly only in the Gauhati Zoo. It is very ugly,' he replied, as he puffed on his cigarette.

'You are also like the Lakshmi owl. When you take Lakshmi around with you, looks are bound to suffer.'

Sheal Babu laughed. He was short and dark complexioned. His face was pockmarked from having suffered from smallpox. When he had stopped laughing, I asked, 'Why is the road in such a bad condition?'

'Tell me, why shouldn't it be bad? It is carrying a much greater load than its capacity. Every day hundreds of military trucks pass through it. War is about to break out,' Sheal replied.

I was reassured. The stronger that Bangladesh's struggle for liberation grew, the worse would be the condition of the road. I looked at Bagaitkar. He had, in the meantime, alighted from the Jeep, and was buying bananas and other stuff. He did not eat rice. Who knew if rutis or chapaties were available in Sheal's shop? I asked Sheal to organize some food. He took the responsibility of arranging for rutis for Bagaitkar. When he informed us that organizing the food would take a little time, I asked him, 'Sheal Babu, did anybody called Pulin Babu come here?'

Sheal Babu was taken aback. After a pause, he said, 'No ...' After another brief silence, he asked, 'Who is this Pulin Babu?'

'A leader from Bangladesh.'

'Why didn't you say that to begin with? Just a minute, I'll make enquiries. There is an office near here.' Saying this, Sheal made arrangements for the food and within a couple of minutes, took me along with him to a nearby house.

2

The door was shut. A girl opened it on our knocking. Her hair was loose. It poured down her back like a black river. She was full faced and of wheatish complexion. In her eyes were vivid streaks of lightning. She wore a blue sari.

'What do you want?'

Sheal Babu was taken aback. It was only natural that he should be surprised. The girl had a kind of dry resolve about her. Her behaviour seemed unnatural. He said, 'Pardon me. I have brought this gentleman along.'

The girl turned to look at me. Unable to bear her piercing scrutiny, I looked downwards. I had had no idea before this that a girl could have such a penetrating gaze. Probably even Surpanakha had not looked at Lakshman in this way. Of course there was no element of lust in this girl's gaze. She seemed to be examining me. After a short pause, her face cleared up, like the sky after the rains. With a faint smile, she asked, 'You are Robin Babu?'

I felt as though the sky was within my reach. I looked at her face, her soft lips and said with relief, 'Yes! Is Pulin Babu in?'

'No. He won't be coming before evening. Where is Bagaitkar?' she asked in a manner that implied that she knew everything.

I replied, 'He's around. He's got down from the Jeep and is shopping. So Pulin Babu isn't coming with us?'

The girl said, 'Come inside with Bagaitkar. I will tell you everything. I have kept some rice and rutis ready.'

I replied, 'We have arranged to have our lunch at Sheal's shop. Don't trouble yourself.'

'Trouble!' the girl said with a wooden smile. 'I don't know the meaning of the word, trouble. Do I look like that to you, as though this is too much trouble for me?'

I was startled. I looked at the young woman carefully. Yes, she was right. Nowhere in that figure was there even a tiny hint of luxuriousness, of lazy habits. Exactly like my wife, Maloti. Maloti was a little shorter than this girl, but there was no sign of laziness or slothfulness either on her. She did not have an inch of superfluous fat on her body. A hardworking girl. Such girls always reminded me of the pitilessness of our world. As for me, I have always looked for a sign of charm and abundance in girls. Women should be able to give men a clue to the mysteries of the world through their body language and by their way of talking. Touching them, or by looking at them, every man should be able to say, 'I have achieved the greatest success and self- realisation.'

Just as Maloti always reminded me of domestic concerns, in the same way, this girl brought to my mind the smoking guns of the battlefields of Bangladesh. A woman's body should have the power to bring to the mind of a man an exquisite and enchanting consciousness of life, free from the sufferings of war, the travails of death and the harsh hardships of this world.

I replied, 'Yes, certainly. Looking at you, people will say that you have brought the consciousness of hard work to a visible, physical form. But then what does Sheal have to say about my eating here?'

Sheal gave a hearty laugh and said, 'For sure you will prefer food cooked by Annapurna herself to that cooked by my Hindustani cook. All right, I shan't ask for damages.'

Listening to this banter, the girl suddenly seemed to be bored. She lowered her head and doodled on the ground with her big toe. I felt as though she was writing the verdict after court marshalling Sheal on charges of disrupting the peace.

Both of us went to Bagaitkar and told him all that had happened. He said with finality, 'Feed our driver here, we will go there.'

Looking at the floor, walls, roof and the kitchen of the house, I got the impression that it was quite old. It was a two-roomed house. The kitchen was a little distance away from the main house. In one room was a photo of Sheikh Mujibur with his hand raised when he was giving a speech. He was wearing a very familiar Jawahar coat, a pair of pyjamas and a pair of thick glasses. It was of an emotional mood that could easily inspire. Back home in Gauhati, I had seen many pictures of the Sheikh in newspapers, but those did not have the emotional pull and the attraction that this one had.

Bagaitkar glanced at the picture, but did not pay any particular attention to it. He examined the table minutely. There were two papers from Bangladesh. He read their headlines very carefully. After this, he sat down on an easy chair and looked at his watch. Then he closed his eyes as though he was meditating and seemed lost in thought. After a while, he said, 'Robin Babu, see, Roumari has been liberated. I see that there is good work being done in Rongpur and Mymensingh.'

I said, 'I can't make any kind of estimate unless I have a map.'

Bagaitkar looked all around the office. There was no sign of a map anywhere. I shifted my gaze once more to the picture of Mujibur. My mind wafted to Bangladesh, the land of beauty–with trees and greenery filled with rivers and waterways. Today, at the sweet touch of this land, the minds of seven crore Bangla people had been awakened. The essence of what Mujibur was saying to them was, 'We shall not remain in bondage to another. We shall not put a noose around our necks mistaking it for an ornament.'

Bagaitkar took out a small map from his pocket, which he had cut out from a newspaper. He became engrossed in looking for Roumari. I sat there and observed him. I thought of Bagaitkar's mind, now focused completely on what he was doing. Suddenly, I was disgusted with myself. Shame on me, what was I doing? The flood had come and drenched all minds. The minds of the Assamese, too, were restless. But like the Ganga, which had been hemmed into a cave, this flood, too, was awaiting the arrival of some Parasuram to cleave a passage through the mountains so that it could flow free.

After a while, Bagaitkar said, 'Roumari is a very small place on the periphery. It is separated from the rest. Therefore, the liberation of this place is not really of any great significance.'

Bagaitkar put the map back in his pocket and remained silent. After a while, he said, 'I have returned from the Akhaura area yesterday. The Mukti Bahini (the armed forces) is well prepared there. They attack at night and return in the morning. Our jawans are helping them with large mortars and machine gun ammunition. The young men are extremely emotional, enthusiastic and also needy. They lack almost everything. But our government is making a mistake. They are encouraging Pakistan to inflict torture and pain on them.'

I replied, 'Indira Gandhi says that she will make the necessary arrangements at the proper time. Be patient. Neither you nor I know the first thing about the science of war.'

Bagaitkar smiled. 'My heart breaks when I see their sufferings. I'm tired of just waiting around. The youth of Bangladesh are fighting a guerrilla war, but they are not yet able to liberate any region. The Pakistani Army will attack after the rains are over. Things will become even more difficult then.'

I laughed and repeated, 'Be patient.'

Bagaitkar became subdued. The girl entered, and said, 'Come, I've served the food.' Bagaitkar looked at her, and said, 'Bhonti, sister, who stays with you here?'

The girl replied, 'Many people come here. But they don't have the time to stay. Most of them go and stay in the refugee camps.' She paused and then continued, 'Eat your food first. We'll talk later.'

Both of us went and sat at one end of the table on the veranda. The table had been beautifully laid. The veranda was quite large and eye-catching. It had a smooth floor and was a little distance away from the kitchen. Our food was laid out on a clean tablecloth. There were chapatis for Bagaitkar and rice for me. She had not served Bagaitkar the fish curry. For me, she had served the fish curry attractively, placing it in a covered bowl in a corner so that its aroma would not assail Bagaitkar's nostrils. There was curd, bananas, mint chutney, slices of lemon, mango pickle, lentils and fried potatoes arranged to perfection for both of us. There was drinking water too in its appointed place.

Bagaitkar was surprised at first. He then took up a ruti in his hands and said with a satisfied smile, 'How did you know that I am a vegetarian?'

The girl, standing as straight as the sapling of a nahor tree, replied, 'I have arranged things in exactly the way Pulin Dada had told me to.'

I questioned, 'When did you say Pulin Babu would be coming?'

'Evening, he said. But you can assume that evening could mean night.' The girl's loosened hair lay quiescent. There was no change in her expression.

I asked Bagaitkar, 'Will we stay here till nightfall?'

'Let's go to Pulin Babu first and bring him here. What do you say, Bhonti?' he responded.

'I can take you if you wish to go and meet him. But it will be difficult to bring him away from there. There is a plan to attack a place near Tangail,' said the girl casually. 'You haven't even started with your food. Eat and we will talk afterwards.' Looking at me, she asked, 'You haven't even touched the fish...why?'

'This dal is so good. I haven't had my fill of it yet. I am eating such tasty food after a long time,' I said, laughingly.

The girl smiled and responded, 'It's not good to praise anybody so much.'

Her statement clearly showed her character. I understood very well that even though she was young in age, she was quite mature when it came to perceiving the true intention behind a flattering statement. I was curious. I asked, 'What is your name?'

'My name is Mehrunnissa.'

'Where are you from?'

'I'm from Kalihati. I had my home there. It's not there now.' She answered in a serious tone and then turned to Bagaitkar, 'Will you have some rice? It's very good rice. Nolseti, from Bangladesh.'

'I haven't had this rice even once after Partition. All right, give me some. We Maharashtrians have rice as well as chapattis. Probably Pulin Babu did not tell you that,' Bagaitkar said.

'No, he didn't tell me that. But there is no harm done if you try it . . . please eat.' She served Bagaitkar some rice with a large serving spoon. I noticed Mehrunnissa's fingers. The signs of hard work were apparent on them too. The ends of her fingers were thick. Looking at her firm body, I was sure that she must be the daughter of a cultivator. Her bangles tinkled melodiously as she worked. Bagaitkar was engrossed in eating his food.

I asked her, 'Looking at you I get the feeling that you are a farmer's daughter. Is that true?'

'You've guessed right,' she replied, laughing.

Suddenly, she became distracted. Perhaps she had remembered the fertile fields, green and gold and abundant with crops, and the nearby village.

'When did you come here?'

'It's been a fortnight. Perhaps you do not know my father's name... Dewan Amir Ali.' Her face grew sorrowful.

Bagaitkar indicated through his facial expressions that I should not talk to her. I understood. From March onwards, the powerful Punjabis had conducted human sacrifices without any consideration of mercy, compassion or empathy. Looking at the eyes of the silent girl, I understood that perhaps Amir Ali was no longer in this world. My innermost being trembled with an unspoken, inexplicable pain. We were living in horrific times. How could soldiers kill helpless people like this? There was a beast inside every man. These soldiers were Yahya Khan's vultures who ate human flesh.

We continued to eat in silence. I remembered a description that I had seen in the papers. It said that even the fish of the Padma and Jamuna, like jackals and vultures, fed on human flesh. I felt a great disgust. I got up without even touching the fish. Bagaitkar was surprised. Mehrunnissa asked anxiously, 'What is it? Is something wrong?'

Rinsing my mouth, I said, 'Give me a tamol or a paan first. I will tell you the reason later.'

I went and sat in the office. A little later, Mehrunnissa came with the betel nut and paan, and asked me, 'So tell me, what is the matter?'

Before I could even speak, Mehrunnissa's eyes grew moist. I noticed that her tears fell, pearl-like, on the bota on which the tamol paan was placed. I was amazed. Just then, Bagaitkar came into the room and standing very close to the girl, asked, 'Bhonti, my sister, why are you weeping?'

At his words, Mehrunnissa seemed to gather strength. She controlled her tears and said, slowly, 'Robin Babu made me cry. He's right. He's absolutely right.'

Bagaitkar asked me, 'What did you say?'

I told them my reason for leaving the table without touching the fish.

Bagaitkar laughed and said, 'Bhonti, this is nothing. The mothers, fathers, sisters of Bangladesh are today fodder for jackals, vultures and fish. Nobody has any peace today, Bhonti. There will be no peace till Bangladesh is liberated.'

Mehrunnissa replied firmly, 'There will be no rest for us, either. Let me clear the dining table. Please sit . . .'

Mehrunnissa left the room.

Bagaitkar said to me irritably, 'You are really very ignorant. Does one talk about these things?'

Once more, I was uncertain. I asked, 'What was my mistake? I have always made it a habit to speak the truth. I do not think there's ever any harm in telling the truth.'

Bagaitkar did not say anything. I fell into an even deeper uncertainty. I was ashamed at my own behaviour.

After finishing her chores, Mehrunnissa entered the room again. She came and stood very close to me. I breathed in a soft aroma of attar and felt the warmth of her body. I said, 'Sit down. Now let's talk about our departure.'

Mehrunnissa sat down on an adjacent chair. Fixing her sharp gaze on me, she said, 'I had an elder brother. He was just like you. That is why many things came to my mind when I saw you. He is gone as well. They killed my whole family. They set fire to the house when they left. The fault was that Babajan, my father, was a supporter of the Awami League.' The girl paused, and said, 'I really don't know how or why I am alive.'

'I shall be very happy if I can take the place of your brother,' I said. 'But we are fleeting acquaintances. Who knows how, and in which direction, the tide of events will take us all?'

I felt that Maloti would be very happy when she got to know of this girl. She had been very concerned when she had read about the merciless killings in Bangladesh, especially when she had come to know of the inhuman torture that helpless girls were being subjected to. 'Do such people exist even in these modern times?' Along with the ladies group of the town, she had tried to send aid to the suffering people of Bangladesh. But she did not have the time to carry out this task. Besides, the relief committees were controlled by a select group of people. Medicines, blankets, mosquito nets, shoes and so on were most urgently needed. But even these were, for the most part, supplied by official agencies. There was no scope for ordinary citizens to help out. In fact, both of us had had that impression till Bagaitkar's arrival.

But on the day that Bagaitkar came as a visitor to our house, we were forced to change our thinking.

To begin with, Maloti was amazed to see Bagaitkar's bag. Could a man travel in a third class train compartment from one end of the country to another with just a small bag? Not only did he have no bedding, he only had two sets of clothes. For some reason, after speaking to him, Maloti came to believe that Bagaitkar was god-like. He was Damodar himself. He was totally indifferent to his own ease and comfort. Coming into contact for the first time with a selfless person like him, she got the impression that he was a divine being. Bagaitkar was a son of Maharashtra, a social worker, dark-skinned and generous spirited, with salt and pepper hair. Of all his fine qualities, the one that attracted my admiring wife the most was his unstinting sympathy for the suffering men and women of Bangladesh. In her mind, Bagaitkar was the symbol of all that was good and sacred in this world.

She began to look after Bagaitkar in special ways. His needs were very simple. He was in the habit of sleeping on a pallet on the floor. Waking up in the morning, he would wash one of the two sets of clothes that he owned. After his bath, he would have his breakfast and go out for the day. Usually, I would not even have left my bed at that time. It would be at least nine o'clock by the time I was ready for my day's work. In the meantime, Maloti would finish her domestic chores and wait impatiently to serve him.

Bagaitkar, through his simplicity, had not just impressed Maloti. She was also, in a way, his student. One evening, Bagaitkar, Maloti and I were sitting and discussing what the people of Assam thought about the Bangladesh liberation struggle and their uncertainties. Would this struggle remain secular and rooted in the love for their language till the end?

Like Gandhi, Bagaitkar said, 'One step is enough for me. For the last three or four decades, Pakistan's leaders have ruled that country on the strength of the union of blind religious beliefs. Today, in East Pakistan, the religious leaders have understood that the Khans have used Islam as a means of controlling them. In Assam too Muslims will come to realise that, in due course.'

I realized that Bagaitkar lived by faith. Unlike me, there was no uncertainty in his mind over every small thing. Maloti would say that this doubt and indecision had crippled my ability to act. It was for this reason that I was unable to take part in the newly born movement. True, I could not do even a little bit of worthwhile work. In reality, even though I had abilities, I had not been able to put them to work.

This kind of intellectual anxiety was a great weakness of those Asomiya people who wished to act for the betterment of society. No leader had come forward to say, 'The deprived masses of the world unite.' Nobody was influenced in any significant way by the Upanishads or by Marx. They had not made much of an impression on the Asomiya mind. Indeed, nobody even had any kind of single-minded devotion for Sankardev either. The Asomiya mind was completely undecided.

Influenced by Gandhiji, a group of people had undertaken Satyagraha. A few of them had gone smiling to the gallows on the strength of their simple beliefs. Thoughts of detachment and duty gave to the tranquil soul an unshakeable belief in the soul's indestructibility. This gave them the hope that they would return to a free India.

This belief was not held by the educated Asomiyas of today. Forget about a Lenin being born here, the land had not seen even a Gandhi or a Kemal Pasha take birth here. Writers such as Dhekial Phukan, Bezbaroa and others like them worked selflessly in the field of Bhasha literature. But the result of this on the Asomiya mentality was that it became harsh and self-satisfied. Even Mujibur's selfless, fearless Bangla nationalism could not give birth to confidence in the mind of any Asomiya. The Asomiya mind did not have the kind of union of economic development, love of the language and progressive Islam that Mujibur had wrought.

Bagaitkar had seen an inexcusable limitation and darkness in my diffident mind. The Asomiya mind was like the dead, stagnant channel of a river. Maloti accepted this criticism of me by Bagaitkar unprotestingly, saying, 'I tell my husband that he is like that cave, or Shiva's matted hair, that holds Jahnobi, the Ganga.'

Sighing, she said, 'If you spend your life in this kind of uncertainty, then your condition will be the same as Bhishma, Dronacharya and others. Even after witnessing Draupadi's humiliation, even after seeing Duhshasan forcibly disrobe Draupadi, the entire assembly remained silent. But what happened in the end? Those Kauravs were destroyed. And Bhishma and Drona were forever branded with disrepute.'

I was Jahnobi, the Ganga! In that case, I had to come out of the matted locks!

Bagaitkar was very impressed by what Maloti said. 'Even an intellectual couldn't have expressed this thought better. It's a fact. This is nothing else but a problem of humiliating people,' he said. On hearing his words, Maloti realized that she and Bagaitkar were like-minded.

Lakhs of refugees had entered Assam. The people of Assam were afraid that because the population had now swollen to unbearable levels, they themselves would be endangered. But this single sentence of Maloti's rendered irrelevant all the agitation and doubts about Mujibur. To tell the truth, after reading the papers and listening to politicians, I had overlooked the actual contours of Bangladesh's freedom struggle. Human beings were in distress. Women were suffering because they were being dishonoured. As soon as I realized this simple truth, I could no longer remain idle. Of my own free will, I set out to work with Bagaitkar. I began to get up very early in the morning. Gradually, I began to feel an unshakeable bond with the freedom struggle of Bangladesh.

When Bagaitkar asked me to accompany him to Tura, at first I responded, 'I'll think about it.' But Maloti said, 'What's there to think about? Since Jahnobi has already burst its banks, let her flow unimpeded. In that country, the Brahmaputra and Ganga meet to form a vast waterway which eventually falls into the sea. You will also be able to go to that country if you go with him now. Go, pay your obeisance to that sacred land.'

Mehrunnissa said, 'But what's the point of simply staying alive? The country is having difficulty surviving. Siddiqui has established a guerrilla force in our Tangail area. I too have worked a bit there. This house that you see was a relief camp for the wounded who had been brought in from the Rongpur area. It's been a couple of days since relief camps were established at the border. The war has grown bigger and so has the numbers of wounded. And so, my work here is done. Where did you say you were going?'

I guessed the girl knew something about nursing.

Bagaitkar answered, 'We need to go to Tura.'

Mehrunnissa smiled and said, 'Yes, you surely will. Let Pulin Babu come back.'

I felt that through this short reply, Mehrunnissa was giving us an order. Perhaps there was more work to be done in Mankachar, rather than in Tura. Bagaitkar asked, 'Didn't Pulin Babu say that there was no need to go to Tura?'

'No.'

Bagaitkar closed his eyes and appeared to be deep in thought.

Mehrunnissa paused. She then said, 'It's not very late. I've been told to wait here till three.'

'Is somebody coming?'

'Yes.'

There was silence once again. Mehrunnissa said, 'You can take a nap if you wish. The beds are ready in the other room.'

'No, we shan't sleep,' replied Bagaitkar. 'Sit down, let's chat.'

'Really, I am hardly fit to join in any kind of conversation with the likes of you. All right. So what relief materials have you brought?'

'Medicines, cotton vests, lungis, mosquito nets,' said Bagaitkar.

'How much?'

Bagaitkar smiled. 'A little bit of everything.'

'Great. Such a huge country, yet they send just a little bit,' replied Mehrunnisa. We had to laugh.

'We are definitely not satisfied with the amount we are giving,' I said, 'but what the government is giving is certainly not a small quantity.'

Sighing, Mehrunnisa replied, 'No, it's not a small quantity. But when you go there, you will see . . . it's just need, need, need everywhere. We have so much shortage and scarcity. Only Khoda can help us.' She continued, 'I know that Khoda is on our side.'

'How do you know that?' I asked.

'I had a dream last night. The muezzins were giving the call to prayer at the Kalihati Masjid. The call sliced across the villages, through the fields and the huts. That call reached my ears. Khoda exists. He does. Will He be able to tolerate this tyranny?'

Once more, I felt the strength of belief. I could not look with suspicion at this Khoda who gave this kind of strength to the victims of tyranny, to the helpless.

It was the same with Maloti's beliefs. After the Kauravs had conspired to disrobe Draupadi, Sri Krishna had told her, 'Daughter of Drupad! Those who have tried to humiliate and dishonour you in this manner will in due course meet a violent, bloody end on the battlefield. I vow that I shall render all help, in all ways possible, under any circumstances, to the Pandavas. The skies might fall, the seas might dry up, but I will be firm in this vow. This is an unshakeable truth.'

As soon as I related this tale to Mehrunnisa, her unhappy eyes lit up. 'This is from the *Mahabharat*. There was a Brahmin Pandit in our village. He taught us in our school. The Pandit had a daughter, Malobika. I heard this story from her. It's true! There were so many heroes, so many learned men in that assembly, yet nobody stopped the act of disrobing Draupadi. It was Sri Krishna who came and rescued her from shame and vowed to destroy those who had humiliated her.'

She paused. It was as though she had seen something, something that terrified her. After a while, she suddenly began to relate a hair-raising but inspiring story. Bagaitkar and I began to listen to her with amazement and curiosity.

3

Morning.

The leaves were dancing in the breeze in the mango orchards. The villagers were preparing to go to the fields. The auspicious sound of the conch shell could be heard in Malobika's house. Dewan had just finished the morning's work, and was getting ready to have breakfast. Malobika had gone to the pond behind the house for her bath. The cows, having been set free, were going towards the forest behind the homestead. The hens were pecking around on the ground in the courtyard. One or two children were walking to school on the path in front of their house.

Suddenly Kamal came rushing in. He said agitatedly, 'Dewan Chacha! Have you heard the news? . . . About Dhaka?'

Dewan Amir Ali had finished his breakfast, and was sitting on a reed mat in the front room chewing a paan. Kamal, too, sat down. For a long time, Dewan kept looking at Kamal without saying anything.

Stroking the beard which signified his many years of experience, Dewan said, 'Kamal Bhai, I have not heard anything. But I know what has happened.'

Kamal looked at the old man with a pitying glance. The terrors that the Khans had unleashed till then were nothing compared to what was happening now. He had no words to describe those terrible massacres. Kamal then looked sharply at the old man and said, 'In Dhaka, they are killing people as though they were cattle or deer. They are using everything–machine guns, rifles, tanks. The Hindus of Sandari Bazar are practically finished. The Khans, the West Pakistani soldiers, have entrenched themselves there. The signboards are in Urdu now. And in Chokoripotti, Rayer Bazar, Nayer Bazar, Polipara, all the houses have been razed to the ground. All the students, the professors of Dhaka University–they are all finished. It's still raining bullets in Jinjira and Narayanganj. The policemen in Gusan are being beaten up. The Kalibari in Ramna is completely gone. They had never harmed anybody. People are fleeing. They chase them and kill them. There are corpses everywhere–they are piled up all over. Sheikh Sahab . . .'

'What's happened to Sheikh Sahab?' Dewan Sahab broke in, in an agitated voice.

'I heard he's been taken prisoner. They've taken him to Pakistan it seems,' replied Kamal. 'This is no time to be sitting around, Dewan Chacha. I hear that they are coming this side.'

'They are coming here?' Dewan Sahab was perplexed.

'Yes,' said Kamal. 'They are wicked . . . they are monsters. Dewan Chacha, people have to be warned. I hear that Abdul Motin is helping them. They are eyeing Poramati, Bhuyanpur, Shimona, Matikota. They are looking towards us. It's time to act, Dewan Chacha.' He got up.

Chachi came out at that moment. Flowers gleamed on her blue sari. She was Dewan's second wife. Sairabanu had been listening to what was being said. Seeing Kamal, she said, 'Kamal Bhai, we have to leave the village by today itself. Habib came and told us. There's no time to sit and think about it. There are girls in the house. It's time for us too to protect ourselves.'

Kamal paused and looked at her. Sairabanu was with child–Dewan Saheb's child. The older son Muhiuddin was in Dhaka. There was no news of him. Who knew whether he was still alive? Mehr and the coming child had to be saved at any cost. Sairabanu's face glowed like the bright clouds at the end of the monsoon season. As for Mehr . . . She was in the full bloom of youth. If those powerful, lustful Khans from West Pakistan saw her . . .

Kamal feared to think along those lines. He worked as a tailor. There was nobody who did not know Kamal in this area. He was famous around here for his work. He was famed even more for his nature. It was generally known that he had wished to marry Mehrunnisa. But Mehrunnisa had not agreed. He did not know whether Mehrunnisa had chosen another person. In any case, he did not like to dwell on those matters. Dewan, too, was a little hesitant in giving his daughter in marriage to Kamal. They were Syeds. Kamal's lineage was not as distinguished.

As he looked at Sairabanu's glowing face, Dewan's grew worried. He asked, 'Is Habib here, Kamal?'

'No. I haven't met him since he joined Qader Siddiqui's group,' replied Kamal.

Confused, Dewan Saheb remained silent for a moment. 'We will have to go far away from the Jamuna, Kamal. But where? Assam? Even that's a three-day journey. I hear many people have gone there. We should also go . . .' said Dewan. 'It is not safe to stay in Kalihati. Let's go and meet Habib. And we will warn the villagers. We'll have to decide something by afternoon.' The old man got up. He picked up a stout stick from the corner beside the doorway. Both Kamal and he walked out swiftly.

Mehr was combing her hair in her bedroom after her bath. Sairabanu went to her and said, 'Mehr, we'll have to pack up our things. Perhaps we will have to leave this place.'

Mehr was surprised. Looking at Sairabanu, whom she called Xoruma, Younger Mother, she asked, 'Where are we going, Xoruma?'

Gazing downwards, Sairabanu said seriously, 'The Khans, those Pakistani soldiers, are coming it seems. They are shaitans, evil. They do not fear committing any sin, any gunaah. It's not safe to stay on here, you know, Mehr.'

Mehr understood what fearsome act her stepmother was referring to. She asked, 'Will Malobika and the others be leaving as well?'

'Yes, they're all leaving. Nobody will stay behind.' Sairabanu's face grew pale with terror. 'Haven't you heard what they are doing in Dhaka? They are killing people indiscriminately. I'm very worried about Muhiuddin.'

Mehr replied, 'Khoda has not gone away, you know, Xoruma. He will protect us.'

Sairabanu did not respond to that. She said, 'Come, Mehr, let us pray, let us offer namaz together.'

Mehr finished tying up her hair and came out with her stepmother. Kneeling in the inner courtyard, they cleansed themselves ritually and prayed fervently.

Mehr did not know how long both of them stayed there. She got the feeling, though, that Khoda was giving them courage from above. She felt stronger in her heart. After she and her stepmother ate a bit, she silently began to gather together their belongings. Later, they went to the kitchen and prepared some food.

For a long time, there was no sign of Mehr's father. Suddenly, teardrops appeared in the merciful monsoon clouds of the month of Saun. A cool draft came in through the door and the windows. On the table in Mehr's room was a pair of bride and bridegroom dolls. The pitiless, brisk gust pushed the dolls to the floor. The fire in the kitchen suddenly leaped up, assuming the greedy form of the lolling tongue of a demoness in the fables. When she heard the dolls falling, Sairabanu's clear complexion, the colour of jute, grew pale.

The villagers had gone to the fields to harvest the jute crop. Abdul, the boy who worked in their fields, had come in the morning and taken the *dao* from the roof of the shed where it had been thrust for safekeeping. He had watched the theatrical performance, the jatra, the whole night in Tangail. He had come on a boat and alighted at the river ghat. By the time he had reached their house, it was quite late. Her father had scolded him. While giving him his breakfast, Mehr had asked, 'Which jatra did you see, Abdul Dada?'

Abdul's face grew as ruddy as the hot vessel in which cane juice was boiled to make molasses. A new kind of jatra had come to Tangail this time. Previously, the jatras would show badshahs and Muslim heroes. Shahenshah Babur, Siraj-ud-Daulah, Mir Jumla—these were the heroes of those folk theatres. It was different now. It was now the turn of the Soviet hero Lenin. Amazing! It showed how Lenin fought against the landowners and capitalists and freed that country. This play, the jatra, was created by boys from Dhaka.

Abdul said, 'Mehr Bhonti, I really liked watching it. Who thinks of the workers of this world?' He paused and then continued, 'Many boys had come. They were saying that Bangladesh also has to be freed in that way.'

Mehr had already heard what Siddiqui and the others were talking about. She asked eagerly, 'I believe they are going to fight?'

Abdul paused. After a while, he said, 'Yes. They surrounded the Khans and killed many of them several times on the Tangail-Mymensingh road. Three hundred and thirty one Khans died in the Kalihati embankment. They have taken away their rifles, arms and ammunitions too.'

He continued, 'I met Habib. I couldn't even recognize him at first. He was in a lungi. He had a beard like a mullah. He said that they have a centre in the jungles. They are training for battle. They are only sowing the seeds now. It will take a while for the crops to ripen. On the other hand, the Khans are infuriated. The Awami League has a strong presence in our village. That's why the Khans might attack us at any moment. Many of their soldiers are coming. They are heavily armed.' After a pause Abdul added, 'Be careful, Mehr. Up at the Brahmin's house, they are packing up. They are going to Hindustan.'

'They are leaving?' Mehr's face fell.

For a long time, neither of them spoke. The leaves of the mango, jackfruit, the jolphai and the banana plants in the backyard swayed in the breeze. The forbidding brow of the monsoon clouds lowered over them. Flying to the top of a tall coconut tree, a bird surveyed the village anxiously. In the forests, the birds, usually quiet, opened their hooded eyes and shrieked loudly in a fearsome way.

'What will you be doing, Abdul Dada?'

Abruptly, Abdul said, 'I will stay. Where shall I go? Kings will come, kings will go. We workers will have to remain. There's no solution.' Sighing, he said, 'So many nawabs and rajas have come and gone in Dhaka. Now it's the Khans who are sitting on the throne there. When Pakistan was created, they said, "It's the Hindus who are at the root of all our troubles. If we can get rid of them, Muslims will prosper." The Khans became the rulers. They chased away the Hindus. But did the Muslims become prosperous? Our fate did not change. Now Mujibur Bhai is saying that the Khans are at the root of all our problems. The Hindus and Muslims of Bangladesh will benefit if they leave. We shall have to fight, wage war, do whatever is necessary. We shall have to lay bare our fields. If necessary, we shall have to die. What's the use of running away? Whatever is fated to happen, will happen.'

Mehr was saddened. Suddenly, there was the sound of thunder. She had heard that the Jamuna was in spate. She asked, 'Have you got any news from Dhaka?'

'Yes.'

Abdul paused again. His eyes too grew sad. He said, 'Banglas are being killed like cattle or deer. Women are dishonoured. They are committing so many sins, so much wickedness, all in the name of Khoda. Why should Khoda tolerate all this? The day of Judgement is coming for them soon, Sister Mehr Bhonti. The King should be careful about what he wears, eats, the way he lives. But what are these people doing? Subjugation, tyranny, persecution. Somehow, we will have to avenge this.'

'What will you do?' asked Meher.

'I shall have to join the Bahini.' It seemed as though Abdul suddenly saw a path open up clearly before him. In some corner of his bewildered mind, there was some hope, some thought of revenge. Perhaps he himself had not been aware of it. Nobody likes to live without hope. He added, 'Habib and the others have done the right thing.'

Mehr asked, 'What are the girls doing?'

Abdul was surprised. He asked, 'What will they do?'

'Shall we remain quiet even after they dishonour us like this? Even the men can't do anything. Tell me Abdul Dada, how will it be if the girls begin to fight?'

Abdul was astonished. What was Mehr saying? It was unheard of. The girls' place was in the home. How would they fight? He replied, 'Fighting is not for girls, Mehr. The only way out for you is suicide.'

Abdul spoke like a very wise person. But Mehr was not satisfied. In the past, women would kill themselves rather than fall into the hands of the enemy and suffer dishonour. She was thinking of another solution altogether.

Abdul left. But Mehr remained worried. If there was any way to get back at them, to avenge this wickedness, she was quite willing to do it. She had heard the stories of molestation. They raped women as though it was their right. When women were dishonoured like this, even their own men looked at them critically and rejected them.

In all her life, she had heard only one story that was a little different. Her stepmother Sairabanu was from Noakhali. When she was young, Ghulam Sarowar's men had tyrannized the Hindus there.

There was an infamous goon in Noakhali called Qasim. Between the two of them, there was no wickedness that Qasim and Ghulam Sarowar did not commit. Gandhiji's Sewa Dal followers had established a camp there. They had stood by the Hindus and supported them fully. After that, a few women had gathered up their courage and confronted the goons. In Sairabanu's village, through the efforts of these workers, a protest against the goons had been organized. Qasim's people had threatened many people there, but the people put their faith in God and stood up unitedly against them.

The Hindus near Sairabanu's house had worked together, collectively. Together, the people had repaired a ruined temple . . .

. . . Sairabanu's grandmother had been a Hindu. Sairabanu's mother's name was Kanakchampa. Her father had been killed by Ghulam Sarowar's people in front of her eyes. Kanakchampa had been forcibly taken away by them and married off to a Muslim teacher. Kanakchampa's name was changed to Alimunissa. Sometime later, she had gone to visit her mother. Her mother had not shed a single tear on seeing her daughter.

In the meantime, Pakistan had come into being. Many people had told Sairabanu's grandmother to go to Hindustan, but she did not. She wished to breathe her last in the land of her ancestors. As Alimunissa was leaving, her mother had said to her, 'You know, Kanakchampa, these people will have to atone for this sin one day. Don't be frightened. One day, they will realize the terrible thing that they have done.'

Alimunissa had asked, 'Ma, will I ever be saved?'

Asking her to come closer, the older woman had said, 'I can't say. I don't know why God made woman so weak when He created her. The condition of the Rajput women is ours too. So many women, like Padmini, killed themselves by sacrificing themselves in a group, rather than fall into the hands of the enemy.'

Alimunnissa had then said, 'I too shall poison myself, Ma.'

The older woman was dumbfounded. She was silent for a long time. At last, she said, 'When Gandhiji had come here, he had told a story. The story of Sita. Ravan had abducted Sita and made her a prisoner in the Ashoka garden. He could not break this chaste woman's devotion towards her husband even for a day. Hanuman had offered to rescue her and take her away, back to Ram, but she waited for her husband to come and save her. Draupadi was dishonoured, but nobody came to protect her. Only Lord Sri Krishna helped her. These are myths. But since you could not protest as Sita did, your downfall happened. There's no point worrying about it now.'

Alimunissa had wept. Just after the older woman died, Alimunissa left of her own accord, without letting anybody know. Some said she had died, others said that she had run away to Hindustan.

Sairabanu was a two-year-old toddler at that time. Her father had raised her with great care. One day, when she was older, Sairabanu had overheard a neighbour, an elderly woman, talk with her grandmother about the things that she had discussed with her mother. She had concluded that there was only one way to escape from the lust of men. Suicide.

After preparing the food, Sairabanu went to the courtyard. Near the heaps of jute were a few chickens, clucking as they pecked around. She chased them away, and then, sitting on a cane murha, looked towards the backyard. She gazed first at the banana plants on which several hands of bananas were ripening. They had planned to cut and bring in some bunches before Eid. Right next to the bananas was a huge tamarind tree. The ground beneath it was so clean that it was possible to eat off the ground itself. Next to it was the pond, teeming with many varieties of fish. On the bank of the pond was a patch of sugarcane. Beyond this were many kinds of trees. On the other side was the boundary of the yard. Across the boundary was a huge graveyard. The lines of graves stretched out till the far distance. Beyond the graveyard was a vast forest.

Sairabanu beckoned to Mehr and said, 'Do you see that forest, Mehr?'

'Yes, I do.'

Mehr examined her stepmother's face. Perhaps she was thinking of going and hiding in that forest. It was a safe place. But safety there was uncertain. People did not enter that jungle even in the daytime, how could they stay there at night?

Sairabanu sighed and said, 'Qader's forces have established their camp there.'

Mehr was surprised. She glanced at the forest and asked, 'How do you know?'

'I know. Your father told me. Nobody knows about it, but I do. It's dangerous to know these things. The Awami League has many enemies. In fact, even Kamal does not know about it.' Sairabanu smiled and continued, 'Habib had come in the morning to take some rice. He's the one who told us that the Khans are approaching. Therefore, we have to flee this place today itself. Your Baba knows all about it. The Khans may even come tonight. Your Baba is advising the people to flee.'

To Mehr, it was all like a story. She was not upset on hearing about the guerrillas. But she still had her doubts. She asked, 'But Xoruma, the Khans are advancing, destroying everything in their path. Will these people be able to save us?'

Sairabanu did not reply. She, too, feared the same thing. Suddenly, Mehr said, 'I have decided. If required, I will kill myself. I shall never allow myself to fall into their hands.'

Sairabanu did not say anything.

Dewan returned after a while. Sairabanu went to serve him lunch. After washing up, Dewan offered namaz and prayed for a long time. It was only after this that he sat down for his food. Sairabanu asked, 'What's been decided about leaving this place?'

'The roads are blocked. The Khans have come. They are waiting,' Dewan replied. 'It's not possible to go towards Madhuban. There's no point going to other places either. They are using helicopters for surveillance.'

'In that case, shall we go into the forest?' asked Sairabanu.

'They've gone from there.'

'Gone! Why?'

'They are guerrillas. They don't have the strength for a direct confrontation. The Khans have found out about their camp. They have left. I shall be going out again. Let me see what can be done . . .' Dewan finished his lunch. He then said, 'I shall return as soon as possible. Yes. Khoda exists. Don't be afraid. I'll be back, soon.' Saying this, Dewan Sahab left.

Even though they sat down to eat together, Sairabanu did not tell Mehr this astounding, fearsome news right then. After they finished their meal, Mehr asked, 'Where has Baba gone?'

'He'll come back soon. The Khans have come. The roads are blocked.'

Her stepmother could not say more. Looking at her face, Mehr saw that it was distraught with terror. She herself felt very apprehensive. She could not depend on her stepmother anymore. After they had finished their meal, both of them went out to the courtyard and sat facing each other. Cautiously, with dread, they offered namaz again. After that, Sairabanu remained silent and fearful for a while.

When the silence grew unbearable, Sairabanu said thoughtfully, 'I shall not kill myself. There is a child in my belly. It will be a sin if the baby is killed.' She paused and then continued, 'It is up to Khoda, let Him do as he wishes.' She kept quiet for some more time, then stood up and said, 'Mehr. We do not have any kind of shield against the lust of men. I keep remembering Ma. You know, I feel that Ma too took her own life.'

'Then what are you afraid of? It is better to die than suffer shame and humiliation,' said Mehr.

'No, Mehr. I cannot kill the child in my belly,' Sairabanu replied. She became silent. Then, understanding Mehr's thoughts, she asked suddenly, 'Aren't you afraid of dying?'

'No,' said Mehr in a firm voice.

Sairabanu smiled and said, 'That's up to you. But it is not right that a child's life should be extinguished. Have you ever heard of a pregnant woman taking her own life?'

Mehr did not reply.

Once more Sairabanu said, 'Sita tolerated all kinds of cruelties in the Ashoka forest, in expectation of Ramchandra's arrival. He did arrive one day. Lanka, the golden land, was reduced to ashes. You know what happened to those executioners who subjugated Imam Husain and Qasim. The same thing will happen to these people too. Bibi Fatema, Bibi Sakina, Bibi Sahrabanu lost everything. Will

Khoda forgive the sins of Yazid? Never. He will never do that. We have nothing to fear if we stay on the path leading to Allah.'

Mehr did not completely believe this. In her mind, she decided what she would do. No matter what happened, she would not run away. Suddenly, she remembered Malobika. Had they gone, or were they still around? She left her stepmother and went outside to find out.

Malobika's house was about a furlong or so away. She walked hurriedly till she was near it. Suddenly, she realized that the house was ablaze. She stopped and entered another house nearby. There was nobody there. Perhaps they were all hiding somewhere. No, they had probably fled. She walked right into the courtyard at the back. From here, she looked at Malobika's house, but she could not make out anything. Back on the path, she heard some people say something.

And then, suddenly, the unimaginable happened. The sound of gunfire. From about four feet from where she was, bullets whizzed towards the courtyard of Malobika's home. There was the sound of constant firing. Stunned, she looked around, but could not make out what was happening.

Suddenly somebody grasped her sari and tugged at it. Her whole being trembled with fear. Terrified, she turned around and saw Habib, clad in a lungi, a pair of canvas shoes and a cap on his head. In his hands was an automatic rifle.

Habib said, 'Lie flat on the ground with your head down. You'll die otherwise. Don't get up.'

Without waiting for her answer, he forced her to lie down on the ground. Habib too did the same, and crawled till he was sheltered by a large banyan tree. He began to fire.

Only now did she realize what was happening. Habib and his group were fighting with the Khans. There was a tremendous amount of noise. She covered her ears with her hands. At one point, either a bullet or a bomb fell on the house that they were sheltering behind. It went up in flames. The firing continued through the blaze.

Suddenly, there was the sound of a Jeep coming. Unable to contain her curiosity, Mehr lifted her head and peered. The Jeep stopped on the road leading to the house. A few men lifted up something onto the bonnet of the Jeep. Probably a machine gun. Long ago, she had once seen something similar in Dhaka. Her elder brother had told her that it was a machine gun. Frightened, she put her head down again.

The machine gun started firing.

After about half an hour, the firing stopped. She was still lying on the ground. Somebody came up to her and whispered in her ear, 'Were you scared, Mehr?'

'No.' She sat up. She saw Habib's bearded face. Blood was flowing from his left wrist. 'What happened to you?'

'A bullet. It's okay. The Khans are finished. We shall wait here for a while. Go and find out about Malobika.' Habib was smiling.

'So you've not left?' Mehr asked.

'We've moved the camp here. We've come here from another place.'

'From where?'Mehr asked.

'You don't need to know. Go.' Habib spoke in a commanding tone.

'Tell me, what's been happening at our house?' Mehr's voice was full of anxiety.

Habib paused, then said, 'You won't break down if you hear the truth, will you? Don't be afraid now to hear this terrible news.'

'What's happened, tell me!' Mehr's heart was thudding.

'Dewan Chacha is dead.'

Mehr felt as though a thunderbolt had struck her. Habib came closer. Holding her hand in his, he said, 'They came just after you left your house. Chacha had gone to the Masjid, where he had exhorted the people to be brave and alert. He had just returned, and was entering his house, when they shot him. I had gone to your backyard after coming in through the jungle. I searched for Sairabanu. I couldn't find her. I heard a terrible scream outside. It was probably Xoruma.'

'What happened?' Tears fell from Mehr's eyes.

'I don't know. I was afraid to confront them. What could I do alone? Besides, my work was not on that side. There were other people who had been positioned there to fight. Surely they were not sitting around idling. You are crying?' Habib held her hand and stroked it lovingly.

'My Babajan is gone, Habib! Who do I have now?' said Mehr. She began to sob.

Habib said, 'You have me, you have your country, you have Khoda. Understand? Everybody in this country is in the same condition. It won't do to cry like a little girl. You'll stay with us from today, okay? Go now and find out about Malobika.'

For a few moments, Mehr took solace in Habib's embrace. She said, 'I trust you. Do you love me Habib?'

'I love you very much,' replied Habib. 'I shall love you even more if you join us.'

'What can I do?'

'We need nurses, Mehr. You will be a nurse,' replied Habib. 'Go now. I will collect the arms and ammunition and get our people together. Come back in five minutes. If Malobika is alive, bring her with you. They have probably finished off her father. Their ancestral temple is also finished. Butchers, monsters, shaitan . . .' Habib cursed them.

Mehr skirted the blazing fires and reached Malobika's backyard. There were four bodies lying in the courtyard. On seeing Mehr, one of them groaned, 'Water! Water! A little water . . .'

Mehr got the impression that this was Karbala. But it was not Hussain's family that was dying of thirst in the Karbala desert. It was the supporters of Yazid who were dying. She felt a surge of compassion. Looking around, she saw a bucket with a little water in it. She brought it and poured it very carefully into the soldier's mouth. The dying soldier drank up the water and then, looking at her, he said in broken Bangla, 'Sister, our place is in hell . . .' He seemed to want to say more but he suddenly lost his voice. Tears poured from his eyes. Mehr felt a sense of compassion and also of curiosity. He indicated that she should put her hand into his pocket. She did so and found a diary there. Inside it was a photograph. At the back of the photograph was scrawled, 'Your Zubeida.'

Gathering all his strength, gasping and speaking in broken Bangla, the soldier said, 'Those who believe in Allah, those who follow the path of belief in the unquestioned supremacy of Allah as the One, those who have integrity, fight in His Name. And those who do not believe in the unquestioned supremacy of Allah as the One are on the side of Shaitan, of Satan. Those who commit injustices are friends of Shaitan. Fight, therefore, against the friends of Satan. In reality, Satan's side is not strong.' (4-76, Quran)

Abruptly, his eyes rolled up. His voice was stilled forever.

Mehr felt as though she had heard these words from the Prophet himself. She really did think that Satan's side was not strong. She looked at Zubeida's picture. She was a very beautiful girl. Her complexion was the colour of peaches, there was a pleasing softness in her face. Her face was as bright and beautiful as a cinema star's. She seemed to be an angel from the heaven.

Suddenly, she heard a groan. Fires blazed all around. The groans were coming from inside the house. The door was open. Concerned, Mehr entered the house. The intense heat from the fires almost scorched her body. The sound was coming from the kitchen. She ran there. The sight that greeted her there made her panicky with terror. The fire was almost upon Malobika's sari, but she had no strength to move away. Mehr quickly lifted her, and rushed outside.

Malobika was unconscious. There was still some life left in her body. Her sari was soaked with blood. She was almost naked. Mehr realized what had happened. She hoisted her up and looked around to see if she could spot Malobika's father's body. Unable to locate him, she came back with Malobika to Habib. Her load seemed to be very light.

Habib was waiting impatiently for her. He was relieved when she came back with Malobika. 'Come, come on. We will have to go in the Jeep.' He had no time even to enquire about Malobika.

It was not safe to be there for too long. He had planned to take the arms and ammunitions with him. Malobika was a slim, delicate and beautiful girl. When Mehr had carried her here, she had felt as though she was carrying the wasted body of a consumptive person for burial. She said, 'Habib Dada, I won't be going. You take Malobika and go.'

Habib became angry. He wanted to leave this place quickly because she was vulnerable. He felt that it was presumptuous for her to be so wilful about this. 'Mehr, have you gone mad?' he asked. 'Even a little delay is dangerous.'

'But I won't be able to leave without finding out what's happened to Xoruma. I am going home,' she said.

Habib did not listen to her. He strode to the Jeep. The machine gun was still fixed on the vehicle. Mehr followed him silently with Malobika and laid her down in the back seat. She went near the machine gun.

Habib lifted the machine gun and kept it in the front seat. He did not look at Mehr. She said, 'You are angry, Habib Dada. I have faith in Khoda. I will be committing a gunah, a sin, if I leave without finding out about Xoruma. You go. Once I know what's happened to her, I'll come to you. You want me to be a nurse, I will be a nurse. You want me to be a guerrilla, I will be a guerrilla. Let me know where I can find you.'

Habib looked at Mehr from the top of her head to her feet. He said, 'I will delay my going for just five more minutes. For you.' He took out a small revolver from his pocket and asked, 'Do you know what this is?'

Mehr looked at the revolver for a long time, then said, 'Yes I do. But what shall I do with this? Will you teach me to use it?'

Habib had hoped for just this answer. 'Come, let's go behind this house. I'll teach you.'

Both of them went behind the burning house. With his hands on hers, Habib taught Mehr how to press the trigger of the revolver. He added, 'Try doing it yourself now.'

Mehr had looked at the revolver with great attention. She took it in her hands and pressed the trigger exactly as he had taught her to. The bullet left the gun with a bang and lodged itself against the trunk of a betel nut tree.

Habib was very satisfied. He took the revolver and showed her how to load the bullets. He then placed the gun, along with a packet of bullets in her hands, and said, 'I am giving you this. It will protect you. Be careful. And go directly on the path to the Garo Hills. I shall give you a card. When you show it, you will be brought to our camp.'

Mehr listened to Habib with great attention. It was afternoon. From the clouds in the gloomy sky came a spattering of rain, like a shower of flowers in blessing. The fires in the houses gradually died down. Mehr could not look very long into Habib's eyes. Many sweet memories surged through her mind.

Habib, too, looked at her face and said, 'I shall always remember you, Mehr.'

'Truly?'

'Yes.'

Overcome, Habib embraced her and kissed her cheeks. He then said, 'I'm leaving. We'll meet again.'

And he left.

All around Mehr, Life, Death, Love and Beauty mingled and became one. Before her was Death. The dead bodies of the Khans. Beyond, there was Habib, a symbol of Love and Life. And in Kalihati's surroundings, there seemed to be an indescribable Beauty. Today, it looked even more beautiful than on other days. This perception was the Truth, this perception was Khoda. The rain washed and revived her; it seemed to give her a new life. With the revolver in her hand, she went slowly up the path to her house. All around, houses were still smouldering. But she did not realize till she reached her home, how completely these houses had been gutted.

Her huge house had burned down to the ground. Nothing remained of the heaps of jute, the barns full of paddy, the chicken coop or the cowshed. There was no sign of any of the animals. There was no sign of any human either. The heavy rains pelted down on the burning embers. She looked towards her bedroom. The bride and bridegroom dolls from Tangail had been burned to ashes. Not a single chair or mat remained. Not a picture in Babajan's sitting room remained. They must surely have used something which destroyed everything in a moment. Like a mad woman, she began to look frantically for signs of her father and stepmother.

Her search was fruitless. She called out loudly, 'Xoruma!' There was no reply.

Suddenly, she noticed a large number of vultures perched on the banana plants, on the jolphai, mango, jackfruit, betel nut, xilikha and tamarind trees. One or two of them flew occasionally and touched the water of the pond. She felt as though her heart had been pierced by a stake. She went hastily to the bank of the pond. At one end, two jackals were lying in wait and staring fixedly at something. She went towards it. The jackals did not budge even when they saw her. Strange, these jackals! Suddenly, she saw a corpse floating in the pond. She went up close and looked. It was the body of a female. Naked.

Nothing was left for her to understand. This was her 'Chhotoma', her stepmother, her 'Xoruma.' But where was Babajan? She could not see him anywhere. Perhaps he had been consumed by the blazing flames.

She was afraid to even cry. She thought of herself as a ghost–as one of those apparitions that lived in the cremation grounds.

She was now beyond all grief. To express grief, it was necessary to have to have near ones around to empathize with. They were no more. She had no idea about the whereabouts of her elder brother

Muhiuddin. If he had not been butchered in Dhaka, then perhaps, like Habib, he too had joined the Qader Bahini. It was useless to grieve till she met up with him. All the recollections of Babajan and Xoruma, and their absence; the destruction of the vast compound and their house, full of memories; the homeless domestic animals, now uncared for; the ten- fifteen bighas of land, full of fruiting trees which now looked bare and helpless like a widow; the fearsome loneliness around the fish-filled pond . . . these were relevant only for Muhiuddin and herself. She had no companions even to grieve with. In her mind was the emptiness of one who has lost everything. An unexpressed meaninglessness filled her heart. Her body felt as though it was not her own. Her soul was an empty pitcher. She was now completely in Khoda's hands. The past came down and stopped at her. She felt that there was no foundation on which to build her future. She knew Habib, but Habib was not yet solely hers. There was a soothing, comforting agreeableness in his kiss, but there was no reassurance on which she could depend to give meaning to her life. Only Allah had that power.

She knelt down on the cool grass beside the pond and began to offer namaz as loudly as she could. The light drizzle drenched her body, but her aim was to fill up the empty vessel of her soul. Her soul was as arid as the desert of Karbala. There was no water.

Finishing her prayers, she rose. The jackals and vultures had not left yet. The sun began to set. Gradually, the drizzle thinned. The last bright rays of the sun glowed in the western sky. Placing her entire past in Allah's hands, she slowly began to return from the land of despair to that of uncertainty.

Suddenly, she heard somebody call her name. A clear, deep, unknown male voice.

'Bhonti, Sister Mehr, come here.'

It was not the voice of a butcher or a shaitan, an evil person. And even if it was, she had nothing to lose. Even if an executioner wished to snatch away her life, she would extract a terrible revenge. She did not feel any love even for her own life now. She was even prepared to sacrifice it. Xoruma had been so eager to protect the child in her belly, but after suffering shame and humiliation, she had probably chosen this extreme step herself. This was not the path of Sita. For the helpless, it was the path of deliverance.

Slowly, walking with great gravity, she went to the track which led to her now totally devastated house. There, she saw a tall young man in a khaki dress. His was strongly built. His bright eyes were moist with tears.

She asked calmly, 'You called me? Why? Who are you?'

The man replied, 'I am Qader Siddiqui.'

Astonished, Mehr examined him from head to toe. She responded, 'I have heard of you. Why did you come looking for me?'

Qader looked at her. He could guess her mental condition. He said, 'I have come to tell you about Muhiuddin. He died in Iqbal Hall. Muhiuddin was my friend.'

Tears threatened to gush out of Mehr's eyes, but she controlled herself. 'I had guessed that something like that must have happened to him. I am glad that you came to inform me about it.' She did not feel the need to express her emotions and feelings.

Siddiqui was surprised to see her coolness and fearlessness. He said in a voice filled with affection, 'Bhonti, it is not just you to whom all of this has happened. Many women of Bangladesh are now in the same condition. Ma Bangla needs the sacrifices of many more. I have not come here just to console you and give you the news about your brother. A band of our guerrillas had come here to defend Kalihati. It could not be defended. The village has become a graveyard. But many of their soldiers have been killed. They are weakened.' Siddiqui paused and then continued, 'What will you do here in this graveyard? Come with me. It will be very good if you join the guerrilla forces. This is the time to sacrifice everything for Bangla Ma.'

Mehr listened to his words with attention. Her father had been an important worker of the Awami League. Her elder brother had been even more hard-hitting and aggressive. As a member of the

Students' League, he had established a retaliatory force in Dhaka. But she did not have much of an appetite for politics. She had not even reached the matriculation level at school. Politics was for men, home for women. This was what her father had believed in. Today, she was homeless. A homeless woman had only Khoda to rely on. Nobody else. The war that Habib was fighting was a man's war after all. The ruler would change, but the condition of women would remain the same. Her stepmother's mother had been dishonoured by the men of Noakhali. Her stepmother had been dishonoured by the soldiers, the Khans of West Pakistan. Was there any surety that she too would not be similarly dishonoured? All men were lustful.

She asked, 'Shall we ever be liberated from the lust of men?'

Siddiqui replied, 'It's difficult to answer that question. But what is the harm in trying?'

Mehr remembered her Xoruma.

The clothes on Mehr's body were still damp. Some parts of her body gleamed brightly. It was these bright, appealing parts, capable of arousing desire that always attracted men. Very few men had been attracted to her mind, her soul.

Siddiqui said, 'Who can give freedom to others, Mehr? That is just another kind of bondage, it's not freedom. You will all have to fight for your own freedom. Only then . . .'

She said nothing. She held out the revolver that she had been clutching and showed it to Siddiqui.

'You know how to shoot a revolver?' asked Siddiqui curiously.

'I do. But I've only practiced once,' Mehr replied in quite a normal tone of voice.

'Who taught you?'

'Habib,' replied Mehr.

Siddiqui smiled.

Darkness gradually began to shadow the horizon. From the masjid came the muezzin's call to prayer. Mehr asked, 'Is there anybody left in our village?'

'Yes. They have gathered together in the masjid.'

'What will they do?' asked Mehr.

'The youth will remain. The old people, women and children will go to Assam.'

Mehr thought for a moment and then asked, 'So I will have to leave too?'

'Yes,' said Siddiqui.

Mehr was reassured. She began to ask about the war. 'Will you be able to take on the Khans?'

'We shall have to. We will have to liberate Bangladesh.'

Mehr felt that Siddiqui had great self-confidence. But how had he come by it?

The sound of the call to prayer from the mosque came to her. The fires that had been lit by the butchers in which her father's house and the entire village had been gutted were still burning. The rain came down heavier than before.

As soon as Siddiqui said, 'Come', she began to follow him.

4

Mehr did not know anything about the battle that had been fought at Kalihati. From Kalihati, they went straight to a masjid forty-one miles away, at times by boat, at times on foot. She realized that nobody knew that a guerrilla group existed. On the way, Siddiqui told her that 391 of the butchers had been killed. The guerrillas had captured about 155 rifles, two LMGs, mortars and ammunition from the embankment of Kalihati and the neighbourhood of the village itself. This band of guerrillas was not a large one. At most, there were probably seventy to seventy-five people. They did not have much military training either. Some had been imparted basic training in the camps in the Garo Hills for a month or two. Some had undergone training at the Madhuban camp of the East Pakistan Rifles.

They slept during the day and walked at night. This was the rule for guerrillas. Siddiqui, Habib and the other leaders were not with them at all times. They went to places such as Tangail, Mymensingh and further afield to Rongpur to recruit guerrillas. The secret meetings of the young men were held at night. During the rainy season, the Pakistani soldiers remained in the towns and cities. They could not enter the chars, the sandbars, of the interior areas. This made things easier for the guerrillas.

That night, Mehr, Siddiqui and the others left Kalihati and rested at the mosque beside the road. They were supposed to move on towards Assam.

The guerrillas who had come to escort Mehr and the others to Assam came to know that the Pakistanis were raining bullets from helicopters on the villages around Kalihati. The guerrillas had destroyed all the bridges. A Pakistani reconnaissance patrol had come along the interior pathway nearby to the border post. The guerrillas had been ordered to surround the Pakistani soldiers and exterminate them. They had left along the path from the Garo Hills, clad in their lungis, carrying arms and ammunition at about one at night to create terror.

Mehr and two guards were the only people left in the camp. A river flowed beside the masjid. Its name was Brahmaputra. The stars of the night watched all that took place. They seemed to be angels. They could see into the innermost recesses of her mind. She went out to the river. On the other side, earthen oil lamps glimmered. Cocks crowed. There was a huge banyan tree on the bank of the river. A cow was crouched near its trunk. Mehr sat down on a stump beside it and gazed silently at the nearby ghat.

It was around two at night. A boat came up and stopped there. She still had the revolver that Habib had given her. But she did not feel any reason to be suspicious.

Two farmers had crossed the river. With them were three women. Each one of them carried a bundle in their hands. Alighting from the boat, they came slowly upto the banyan tree. One of them said, 'This is the path. Islampur village is nearby. Go there. Stay there for the night. Then, leave for Assam. It is a day and a half away from here.'

The three women and the man said their goodbyes to him and went towards the village of Islampur. The other man returned to the boat. There was the sound of oars on the water.

A flood of people was going to Assam. People from Mymensingh district were mostly going towards the Garo Hills, a part of Assam.

After a while, another boat appeared. The previous scene was repeated. After that, four more boats came in a similar way. The roosters of the village announced the approach of dawn. Bright colours burst forth on the eastern sky. Mehr thought of Malobika. Habib must have taken her to Assam. She had probably regained consciousness by now, perhaps in some hospital, or in some room at a relief camp. She remembered her Xoruma also. Why did Malobika not commit suicide in the same way as Xoruma's mother had? What a disgusting society they lived in! How much longer would such sins continue in Khoda's holy land? Did the quality of lustfulness exist only among the males of Pakistan? Wasn't it present in men of other countries too? Other men, too, could be lustful, but they were in control. In those other countries, women's bodies and souls were not wronged in the way the Pakistani soldiers were wronging the women of Bangladesh at this time.

In the morning, she went to the river for her bath. The water was still cool. The villagers on the other bank had not yet come to the river's landing place on that side. A lake glimmered in the far distance. She went underwater several times treading the water. She scrubbed herself thoroughly. She then came up to the bank. The two guards were still asleep. She changed her clothes and went to the masjid to pray. She decided to make some tea. It was time for the guerrillas to return. Putting some water on the stove to boil, she looked around and found some eggs and bread. After washing the eggs, she boiled them and sliced the bread. She peeled the boiled eggs and put them along with some salt in a saucepan. She arranged the slices of bread on a large plastic tray and poured the tea into four huge flasks. She looked at the sleeping guards. She did not wake them. Nor did she take any food herself. She sat outside the masjid and opened the diary of the dead Khan, the Pakistani soldier.

His name was Yakub. She remembered his dead face. It was light cream in colour–the hue of the chomchom sweetmeat of Poramati. But it was fresh, like a young palm leaf. There was no way she could find out anything about his native place, his age or who his parents were. It was difficult even to know whether he had been from Punjab or Baluchistan. There was no way either of finding out how long he had been a soldier. He had come to Bangladesh only recently. There was nothing much in the diary either. While turning over its pages, her eyes suddenly stopped at a particular page.

The entry was dated 25th July. That day, they had surrendered control of a small station on the Chattagram-Dhaka railway line. They had gone to a place about a mile away. Sitting beside a machine gun in a bunker, he had written:

> *Her face was like Zubeida's. Exactly the same. Only the clothes were different. Shefali was wearing a sari. She had bright red alta on her feet. Her complexion was exactly that of the half-ripened wheat in our fields, the colour of pale gold. She was trembling. I have never seen anybody trembling like that.*
>
> *I asked her father, 'Where is Ismail?'*
>
> *In a quiet, grave voice, he said, 'I do not know.' Wherever we have gone, looking for their volunteers, the answer is always the same, 'I do not know.' They have all joined Mujib's army.*
>
> *Our Havildar ordered, 'Bayonet the old man.'*
>
> *I was powerless to disobey his command. We are trained to obey. We have no opinions, no minds, no preferences of our own. Nothing. I lifted my bayonet. Suddenly, my eyes fell on Shefali. Even though she was terror-struck, she rushed up and hugged the old man and said to me in broken Urdu, 'In the name of Khoda. Don't kill him.'*
>
> *There is magic in the word 'Khoda'. My bayonet was stilled. It was as though it was Zubeida who was speaking to me, not Shefali. Her voice, too, was the same. I felt as though Zubeida was telling me, 'It will be a gunah, a sin.' I too understood that this was not Jihad, it was not a Holy*

War. It was gunah. A sin.

Somewhere, somebody seemed to be weeping. They had brought us here to protect the country. Why were they telling us now to kill people like this? It's been six months now. We are not fighting against the Hindustani soldiers, are we? We have been killing the Banglas. Fratricide. The killing of brothers. I could not do it.

My bayonet just wouldn't move. I said, 'I can't.'

My superior officer was actually seeking just such an opportunity. His eyes seemed to be on fire. He grabbed Shefali by the hand and took her away from my sight. He ordered my colleague Jamal to shoot the old man. I closed my eyes. The old man did not utter a single sound. He slumped to the ground.

If Zubeida hears of this, she will never forgive me. Shefali . . . I could hear her terrified screams. Whatever had to happen, happened. I was helpless, Zubeida. Dishonour in the name of Allah. Khoda! Khoda! I heard the agony of her body and her final scream before she died.

The old woman was still inside the house. She came out and fell on her husband's dead body. She wailed, she cried. 'Allah! Allah! I have nobody.'

I wanted to speak. Possibly I wanted to tell her, 'You have me.' But did she have me? Was I, 'I' anymore? Am I Zubeida's 'I' now?

Mehr's body shivered with shame, revulsion, terror and dread.

She looked towards the sleeping guerrillas. The sky was overcast. The forest was nearby. The masjid was an abandoned one. Both were sleeping without any worries. They were both lovable lads. One was Sameer, the other Ismail. Sameer had come from Dhaka. He did not know what had happened to his parents or his sisters. He had heard that they had gone to India. But people who had come from there told him that bullets were being rained from the sky on fleeing refugees. If they were alive, they would surely meet when Bangladesh was liberated.

Yesterday, Mehr had asked him, 'Will Bangladesh ever be liberated?' He had replied forcefully, 'It will be. It will. It will.'

But she hadn't yet spoken with Ismail. He was a very shy boy who spoke little. Even though the sun had risen, there was no sunshine. The tall jute plants gleamed in the distant sandbanks of the river. Right next to them were the golden paddy fields. From the sandbank across the river, snatches of conversation occasionally wafted down in the breeze. Mehr thought of Shefali. Her name, Shefali, was a Hindu one, but she was a Muslim. Her condition was even worse than Malobika's. At least, Malobika had survived.

She went through the pages of the diary. Suddenly, like Shefali's mother, her heart began to lament, 'Allah, I have nobody. Allah, I have nobody.' This lament was not hers alone. It was the lament of all those people of Bangladesh who had lost everything, everybody.

She began to turn the pages again. Many pages were blank. She came upon some new notes made on the first of August.

Since that day, I don't know what it is, but a melancholy has settled on my mind. My superior officer is treating me as though I am a kafir, as though I am outside the Muslim faith. This does not frighten me at all.

The other day, something quite outlandish happened. Some semi-naked women were made to advance before our attack unit in order to excite the boys of the Mukti Bahini. Once more, I thought of Zubeida. 'Men of honour fight on the path of Allah. Those who are not men of honour, fight on the path of Shaitan. Those who are unjust are companions of Shaitan. Therefore, Shaitan's side is not strong.' These were not Zubeida's words, but Allah's. But maybe Zubeida was under the impression that I had come in the name of Jihad. But this is not the way of Allah, it is the way of Shaitan.

We crossed the river, and continued. Our feet sank into the marshy land. We were bitten by leeches and gadflies. The superior officer had become a monster, a fiend. Otherwise, how could he use these women in this way? I happen to know why such things have to be done. There are strict orders from above that the Chattagram–Dhaka rail line has to be reopened. There's a plan to destroy the bunkers of the Mukti Bahini today.

> *Gradually, we crossed fields of the dense jute plants. Suddenly, we came out into open the paddy fields. Bullets began to rain from our left, our south and from behind all of a sudden. There was no alternative but to leave the women right there and fight our way back as we retreated. We are waiting for support from the Air Force. But will the Air Force bring victory? Leave aside winning over the people of Bangladesh, we are, on the contrary, sowing the seeds of hatred.*

While she was reading, Sameer woke up. He rubbed his eyes and quietly went down to the river to wash up. Mehr found nothing else of interest in the diary.

She called out, 'Ismail!'

Ismail turned over. He opened his eyes and stared at Mehr. She said, 'I've made breakfast. Get up and eat. The others haven't come yet . . .'

Ismail thought for a while, then said, 'There must be some big trouble somewhere. Otherwise, they wouldn't be so late. Didn't you sleep at night?'

'No,' replied Mehr.

Ismail laughed. 'It's difficult to sleep out in the open, isn't it?'

Mehr looked at Ismail and smiled. The boy was very attentive towards her. He had been noticing with sympathy all that she had done in the last one and a half days. No matter where she was, Ismail would look at her and give her a smile. But she did not feel any urge to converse with him. Her mental state was the same as that of the old woman's described by Yakub in his diary. 'I have nobody.'

Ismail got up and after washing his face, came and sat cross-legged before Mehr. 'Give me my breakfast, Baideo,' he said, addressing her as 'elder sister'.

Mehr asked, 'Where is your friend?'

'He's sitting at the landing on the river and looking at the other bank,' replied Ismail.

'Isn't he hungry?' asked Mehr with a laugh. 'And will you be able to eat by yourself, leaving your comrade hungry?'

'Who's a comrade, who's not, when one is hungry?' said Ismail. 'Sameer is moody, his moods change very quickly and he becomes a different person. He likes to look at the sky, the forests, the river, the fields of paddy and the distant villages. He spends his time staring at them. Sometimes he laughs to himself. Sometimes he groans unconsciously as though there is some deep despair in his soul. But he says nothing when asked. I've never seen such a strange boy.'

Mehr asked Ismail, 'Could it be that he has nobody to call his own?'

'It's difficult to say whether he does or does not. And in any case, who do any of us have to call our own? I've not been worrying about my home since the time I left it. This land of Bangladesh, this soil, is now our mother.

Amar shonar Bangla ami tomay bhalobashi
Tomar akaash, tomar bataash
Amar praney bajay banshi . . .
My golden Bengal, I adore thee
Your skies, your breezes
Play the flute in my heart . . .

At the call of this flute, I left everything behind and came running.'

Mehr exclaimed, 'You love your land so much!'

'Yes. Those who have died are buried in the soil of this land. Those who live, work on this land. I love this land very much,' replied Ismail. 'Now, I'm dying of hunger. Please give me the food first. We'll talk later.'

'Call him also,' she said.

Ismail was about to get up when Sameer appeared. He had neatened his hair. There was a gravity in his walk. In his hands were two dolls. He came and sat near Ismail.

'What have you got there?' asked Ismail.

'Two dolls. Just see, how pretty they are! Somebody dropped them here last night while passing this way.' Ismail placed them carefully on the floor of the masjid. 'Wah . . . How beautiful!'

Mehr placed two large leaves with their breakfast in front of them. She fetched two plastic glasses and filled them up with tea. The dolls reminded her of the figurines in her home. She examined them wistfully. Her attention wandered. Ismail began to eat the bread and eggs. But Sameer did not start. Instead, he took out a pair of conch-shell bangles from his pocket. These were worn by married Hindu women to show their marital status. On the smooth surface of these bright markers of marriage were etched floral designs.

Mehr remarked, 'What a pretty pair of bangles! They must be from Dhaka's Xankhari Patti, the locality famous for making these.'

Sameer said, 'I found these too in the sand. I've brought them for you. Will you take them?' On his face was an expression of boundless eagerness.

Mehr's face flushed. However, she controlled herself and said, 'What shall I do wearing these bangles of conch shell? I do not really like them. Give them to somebody else.'

Sameer seemed piqued. He said, 'I've been thinking while sitting on the river bank. I've decided that this pair of bangles will suit only you. I am not mistaken in the slightest. These dolls and bangles have been given by the Brahmaputra. You sat throughout the night by the Brahmaputra and spoke soundlessly to the river. That is why this gift was given. Take them. We are so many brothers here. We have only you to call our sister, elder or younger, Baideo or Bhonti. Take them. Life dances to the beat of Rudra's tandav, Shiva's dance of destruction. Our lives as guerrillas are temporary like the bubbles on the surface of the Brahmaputra. How many opportunities are there in this uncertain, fleeting life for affection? These conch-shell bangles are a gift from Ma Bangla. The dolls too. I am giving you the bangles. And I shall give the dolls to someone else.'

Ismail was having his breakfast as he listened to Sameer attentively. Now he asked, 'Who will you give them to?'

'Shan't tell you that either,' said Sameer. He placed the two bangles in Mehr's hands. Sameer's words made a deep impression on her. Abruptly, she felt the urge to wear the bangles. But as she was about to do so, there was suddenly a great turmoil in her heart. The words began to echo within her, 'I have nobody, Allah. I have nobody.'

Her eyes grew moist. Ismail guessed what she was feeling, but he said nothing about it. Instead, he said, 'Baideo, it's your turn to eat now. I will serve you breakfast.'

'No, I can get it myself,' said Mehr. 'I don't feel like eating at all.'

Ismail persisted. He said, 'If you say such things again, instead of fighting against Yahya Khan, I shall fight with you.'

Mehr felt a lightening of her heart. She asked, 'Will you kill me or what? I shall be saved if you do.'

'Why should I kill you? I shall undertake Satyagraha. A hunger strike. I too shall stop eating.' Ismail said these words in such a way that Mehr laughed heartily. Gathering up her courage, she managed, this time, to wear the bangles. After this, she said, 'Okay, I'm sitting down. Bring the food.'

Seeing Mehr happy, not just Ismail, Sameer too, was very glad. Everyone in their group had been trying to bring a smile on her face all this while. Today, at last, they were successful.

While having her breakfast, Mehr felt that there was still laughter and joy, love and affection left in the world. The three of them were homeless. Like Bedouins, they had pitched their tent in this isolated masjid on the banks of the Brahmaputra. This game would now come to an end. Nobody could take the place of her Xoruma, her Baba, her Dada, elder brother. She had not got this affection from Habib even when he had kissed her. It seemed to her that Habib was tough, as though, in his heart there was a slab of ice. There was no doubt that Habib had a great deal of affection for her. But his closeness could not bring to her heart a surge of emotion like the waves raised by the wind on the waters of the Padma and Meghna. His love, too, was a nomadic love, that of a Bedouin. Ismail's affection was like the chomchom sweetmeat of Poramati.

The sweetness lasted a fleeting moment. The heart could not rely on it. A new kind of fraternal feeling had arisen in Sameer's mind. He too had probably lost everything, everyone. Like a drowning man, he was clutching at tender shoots of newly sprouted grass. In this situation, there were no differences to separate their minds. The Hindu and Muslim minds seemed to merge in this vast expanse of the Ganga-Brahmaputra waterway. He was trying to bind her to him with these conch-shell bangles.

Nobody asked about others' past here. The past was a vast graveyard.

'When will the others come?' asked Mehr impatiently.

'I'll go and find out,' said Sameer.

'Where?'

'We have our bunker just across the river,' said Sameer. His face grew worried. He seemed to hear something, a rumbling, somewhere. He stood still for a while and listened alertly. He then said, 'Ismail, can you hear it? It's their helicopters.' He paused, 'Bring all the stuff in and close the doors. Let me go and find out.'

The rifle lay in a corner of the large veranda. Slinging it on his shoulder, Sameer walked cautiously towards the banyan tree. Ismail gathered their things together and called Mehr into a room in the masjid. He locked the door from inside.

It was an extraordinary incident. The helicopters were coming from the direction of the Brahmanberiya Cantonment. The sound gradually became clearer. Ismail thought that it would be best to keep the LMG ready. After he had positioned it, he thought it would be better to keep it in a position of advantage. They had surely found out about the guerrilla camps. He took the LMG, opened a window facing the river and lifted it up there. He gestured to Mehr to bring a table. The height of the table was a little lower than that of the window. The mouth of the machine gun faced the river.

Ismail asked, 'Baideo, have you ever fired a machinegun?'

'No,' said Mehr, fearfully. 'Habib had given me a revolver.'

'Keep it with you,' said Ismail.

'Is there any danger?' asked Mehr.

'I don't know,' said Ismail. 'But it's best to be ready.'

Ismail was confused. He could not figure out what was happening. But Sameer would surely give a signal if there was any danger. He began to perspire. Neither of them spoke. They stood and listened to the sound of the helicopter. It was coming from the south-east of the masjid. They were reconnoitering. Gradually, it came above the masjid. The ground and foundations of the building shook. Slowly, Mehr took out the revolver from her bundle. There were several rifles lying around within the masjid, but they were of no use to her since she did not know how to use them.

She realized that Ismail was not looking at her. He was still listening to the sound of the helicopter. Her heart seemed to thud along with that sound. For a moment, she forgot everything. She would have to protect herself. In reality, nobody could actually protect anybody else. People were insignificant given the enormity of events that were unfolding. Very insignificant. She knew what she had to do now. Even if she could not kill anyone else, she would kill herself. The helicopter was still hovering overhead. It almost touched the tin roof of the masjid.

Suddenly, a smile lit up Ismail's face. 'Why is your face so pale?'

Mehr did not reply. She looked down at herself.

Ismail laughed. 'Why are you afraid? We have no alternative except to fight.'

Abruptly, the sound of the helicopter began to go towards the other bank of the river. After a short while, they heard the sound of firing.

Ismail went towards the window. The sound of firing increased. 'They are firing at the bunkers,' he said.

Mehr went and stood near Ismail. She said, 'I understand that. But I am not getting any hope, any reassurance.'

Ismail said affectionately, 'Do you hear the sound of firing? Our boys are fighting very hard and with all their might. Who are we fighting for? We have lost everything, but we have faith in Allah. Our Mother, Ma, is with us.' He paused and then continued, 'Ma. We have a vision, a dream of a new life in Ma Bangla's bosom.'

Esho go notun jeebon,
Esho go kothor nithoor nirob . . .

Come, O new life,
Come, O harsh, cruel silence
Come, O dazzling, O beautiful,
Come, O disliked, bitter, tasteless,
Come, O tearful dampness,
Come, O unadorned, bare body,
Come, O open mind,
Leave aside the beautiful blossoms
Of maloti and malika,
Moonlit nights, misty, magical,
Come, O powerful darkness of unbroken nights,
Heartwarming,
Come, the mighty abode of grief,
Destroying the shoots, saplings of hope,
Come, O war, come O Great Victory,
Come, O certainty of death.

Mehr listened with great attention to each and every word in this song. A song that welcomed a bitter relationship. She asked, 'I haven't understood everything. But I feel all this is just imaginary. It is not something that women can have faith in or confidence about.'

Ismail paused. Nothing–neither their brotherhood nor their guns, the imagination of the world-renowned poet nor even the words of Allah–nothing was enough to reassure Mehr. Women, the women of Bangladesh, had perhaps lost faith in the masculinity of men. His happy smile faded.

On the other side of the Brahmaputra, firing was still going on. Ismail opened the door of the masjid. A cool, soft breeze came in. Ismail became melancholy. They had come from Dhaka and joined the guerrilla forces. They fought alongside the other guerrillas. He had tried to make sense of all that had happened in these last six months, but had not succeeded. What was Ma Bangla? He had experienced the beautiful green forests in the low-lying land which was washed by the vast concourse of the Brahmaputra and Ganga . . . But he could not experience the grief of the women who cowered in the dark huts or of the men who tilled the land and made it yield abundant harvests.

Mehr, too, came out. Looking at Ismail's serious face, she said, 'Look. Do you really believe that Bangladesh will be liberated?'

'I do,' replied Ismail. In a corner of the masjid's courtyard was a jackfruit tree. With a heavy heart, he sat down under it. He gazed sadly at Mehr. What did she want?

Mehr was completely unconcerned. Every now and then, she remembered Malobika. Where was she now? Would she regain her chastity after she recovered? Would the Hindu people, would the Brahmins, ever give her a place in society again? Would Muslim men accept those Muslim women who had been dishonoured? Even if Bangladesh was liberated, its women, particularly its dishonoured women, would not get their honour, their chastity back again. The Pakistani enemy could be killed with a gun, but a gun could never bring back a woman's honour. She did not know what was required to obliterate these age-old traditions regarding women in the male-dominated society.

Mehr looked at Ismail. She felt a sense of revulsion against herself. Ismail and Sameer were very good, honest boys. They wished to look at her as their Baideo, their elder sister. They had succeeded, too. But she had such a suspicious nature! Love and affection could not touch or move her anymore.

She went near Ismail and said, 'I feel as though I have some terrible disease. I have no answers to the questions in my mind.

You know what I think sometimes? It's as though I am looking at everything upside down. I am looking at things through the eyes of a woman.'

The guns were still being fired. But gradually, the sound of the helicopter faded away into the distance.

After a while, Sameer returned. He said, 'Ismail.'

'What?'

'There may be bombers coming in now. They could have defended and retained the bunker if they had had even a single anti-aircraft gun. The Khans can even come by the river.' Sameer paused. 'What is the best thing to do?'

Ismail looked at the sky. There were dark clouds gathering. There might be rain. He was not expecting the bombers to come. But he, too, was worried about the bunker.

He asked, 'Didn't anybody come from the other side?'

'Where? No.'

With deep conviction, Ismail said, 'They'll come.'

Sameer said, 'People must have died there, or been injured.'

'Probably.'

Ismail took out a cigarette from his pocket. Sameer said, 'Give me one,' Ismail gave him that cigarette and took out another for himself.

Suddenly, Mehr asked, 'What are the arrangements for food today?'

'Nothing. There are no arrangements.'

Mehr did not say anything. For a long time there was silence. Ismail was still thinking. How could these guerrilla bands be made into a proper Peoples' Army? Mehr still did not understand the meaning of the sacrifices they had all made. He, too, had not been able to explain it to her.

In a corner of the rain-laden, weeping sky, Mehr seemed to see her Xoruma, Baba and Dada. They appeared to have got wings of cloud and were now flitting about like the birds of dawn. Life and Death had merged and taken a tragic hue.

Ismail was looking at Mehr. In the anchal of her blue sari, he could see a resemblance to his mother and sister. Their lost faces, voices and glances became apparent to him in this mirror.

When fleeing through the paddy fields and swamps under the cover of darkness, all their faces, eyes, words, dreams, fears and sufferings had collected in a pile in one corner of his mind. The smoke from the gunpowder of battle, the heated political arguments and the smoky haze, the untiring efforts at understanding what was happening . . . nothing could touch that pile. Now, in Mehr, he was seeing them all.

Sameer, too, was looking at Mehr. In his mind, Mehr was now a wild, bullet-riddled channel of the Brahmaputra. She wanted to go somewhere, but he had no idea where. His Ma, Baba, sister were now one with nature. Nature had given the conch-shell bangles and the two dolls depicting a bride and a bridegroom. Those bangles on Mehr's wrists seemed to bring an untainted dream. He wished to give her something more, but he could not understand what exactly that thing could be. Maybe he could give a pure being such as a white swan or some soft, unpolluted and unblemished thing.

Nobody really got the opportunity to understand others.

Suddenly, there was the sound of soft footsteps coming from the nearby thicket. They all looked towards where the sound was coming from.

Not too far away, two lungi-clad men who looked like fishermen were staring at them in astonishment. Ismail lifted his rifle. Sameer, too, became alert. Mehr stood up.

One of them spoke. 'Are you Qader Sahab's people?'

'Why?' asked Ismail.

'There's a letter,' replied the other.

'Who has sent it?' Ismail asked.

'Habib Sahab.'

Ismail looked at Sameer. Sameer began to laugh. He kept down the gun and sat on the ground. 'I recognize them. They are from the nearby village.' He beckoned them to bring the letter.

The man came forward and without any hesitation handed over the letter to Sameer. He, too, sat on the grass. He said to his companion, 'Go to the boat. I shan't be going home today. I'll have to take them with me.'

The other person vanished into the thick undergrowth. The person who had brought the letter put down his net and taking the gamosa, handmade cotton towel, from his shoulder began to fan himself with it. Sweat poured down his dark, bare body. Mehr's ears pricked up. Her eagerness to hear about Habib was clearly evident in her eyes and face. And what about Malobika?

Sameer read the letter. His face became gloomy. Without a word, he handed the letter to Ismail. After reading it, Ismail calmly put the letter into his pocket. His face became expressionless. They all seemed to have become dumb. Mehr's curiosity remained unsatisfied.

The man took something made of lead from his hand. He examined it minutely and then threw it far away.

Abruptly, Sameer lay down on the grass. Looking up at the vast, cloudy, sky, he hummed a song

Kanday na, kandey na, Joynal,
Karbalar moidaney
Kandey na, kandey na, Joynal.
Weep not, weep not, Joynal,
In the battlefield of Karbala,
Weep not, weep not, Joynal.

The soft melody sung in the sweet voice brought a shower of rain to the burning, thirsty and tired desert of Mehr's mind. Yazid could not defeat anybody. He was himself defeated. After they had lost everything, Zainab, Fatema and Sakina found the stream of freedom in Karbala itself. Why should she not find it, too?

Ismail came close to Mehr and said, 'Mehr Baiji, sister. We shall have to leave. There's work to be done. You . . .'

Mehr smiled. 'I shall have to stay here alone? Is that what you're trying to say?'

'Yes,' said Ismail. 'Of course there is a village nearby. You can go there if you wish.'

Mehr thought for a moment. 'But then . . . Where do I have to go? I've come here with your group. I've not been able to do any useful work. Habib had told me to become a nurse.'

Ismail's face cleared up. He asked, 'Do you really wish to become a nurse?'

'What else can I become? I can't think of anything else. All right, now tell me, do you know where Malobika is?' she asked.

'No,' said Ismail. 'Where is she from, this girl?'

On hearing about her from Mehr, he said, 'We'll have to find out.'

'Has Habib written anything about me?'

'No.'

'Where is he now?'

'He's returned to Kalihati.' Ismail did not say why he had gone. It was best for guerrillas not to talk too much. Ismail took out Habib's letter and tore it up into little bits.

Mehr's mind filled with a kind of resentment. She said, 'Leave me in Allah's hands.'

Sameer stopped humming. He said, 'Mehr Baiti. There's food, isn't there?'

'Yes, there is.' She silently brought out the containers of tea and the breakfast from inside and placed them before Sameer. 'Since nobody else is coming you eat your fill,' she said.

Sameer said, 'Why should I eat alone. We shall all eat together.' He called the other man, and gestured to Mehr to eat too. As they were about to start, Ismail suddenly asked the man, 'Tell me, is there anybody who's going to Haluwaghat today?'

'Somebody is always going there. Why?' asked the man.

'This girl has to be taken to the camp.'

Mehr had just finished eating an egg. She asked, 'Why are you so worried about me? Leave me in Allah's hands.'

The man said with affection, 'Don't you worry, Ma. Stay the night in our village. There will be people going to either Mahendragunj or Haluwaghat tomorrow. They'll take you with them.'

'How far away is your village?'

'It's on the way.'

'In that case, come with us, Baiti. It's getting late. Our work is urgent.' Saying this, Ismail hastily ate up his food. In the meantime, Sameer gathered up the remaining stuff lying around the camp into bundles. Only the LMG was heavy. Ismail took that.

The man said, 'There are more people a little further away. You will have to slog it out till you reach there.'

The three of them, with bundles in their arms, were ready to leave. But they saw that Mehr was standing still, immobile.

Sameer said, 'Baiti, come.'

Mehr was defeated. She did not wish to go. But she saw no logic in staying behind, either. There was no work for her anywhere. She was simply a burden, an object of pity for men. She could not even find a way to prepare herself for some field of work.

She began to walk in silence, like Sita, going towards Panchabati. But she had nobody with her whom she could call her husband. This journey was for the sole purpose of saving herself.

5

The most valued property of Islampur's farmers, their cattle, were returning to their sheds in the evening, raising the dust on the way home. From distant waterways, the fishermen's boats began to return to the river landings. In the quietude of dusk, gadflies and mosquitoes entered the huts on the earthen embankments and began their bothersome humming.

The young second wife of the elderly householder took their baby under the mosquito net over a bed that was the size of a small house. Quietly, she began to nurse the child to sleep. The clouds roared as soon as the night began to deepen and the wind and rain beat down with a tremendous sound on the roof of the hut. The betel nut trees in the yard fought with the fierce wind like the weak, but brave, guerrillas and fell down, broken. The glutton of a dog, after gorging on rice, burrowed deeper into the heap of jute on which it was lying. Someone singing a melodious Bhaitali to the accompaniment of a dotara in some nearby home grew quiet. The envious complaints at the tip of the tongue of the elder wife, like the vessel of rice coming to a boil next to the flickering oil lamp, became quiet too.

Mehr sat silently on a beautiful split-bamboo mat and thought of Habib. Why had he not written about her? Why had he not sent any news of Malobika?

There was no point in being upset. The guerrilla bands had not yet come face-to-face with the Pakistani soldiers to engage them in battle. They could make the powerful Pakistani Army uncomfortable. They could cause disquietude but could not defeat them. Everybody was full of praise about their bravery. But the helpless people, the aged, the innocent children and feeble women were not reassured.

After nursing the baby to sleep, the younger wife came and sat beside her and said, 'Roushana's father was saying that the Khans are coming by boat.'

Mehr was startled. The woman said soberly, 'If they do come, they will finish everything.' She paused and then added, 'The things we've heard! Such hair-raising stories . . .'

Mehr could not think of anything to say. There was no point in asking either. The army would definitely attack this guerrilla-dominated area. She did not feel like thinking about what would happen to her in the future.

The younger wife continued to talk even though she noticed Mehr's silence. She had to voice her fears. She hardly spoke to her co-wife. Her husband had told her not to talk about these things in the village. There were spies in the village. Therefore, she was not about to let go of this opportunity of speaking her mind.

'About ten days ago, my Mama, my maternal uncle, came from Mymensingh,' she said. 'He said that earlier there were no Khan soldiers there. Now they have entered the place. They search for people belonging to the Awami League and kill them. As for what they do to the Hindus, the less said, the better. The Khans come in groups to the villages. Once the monsoons are over, they will come with tanks.' She paused and then added, 'Roushana's father however says that they will surely lose. Our soldiers will arrive by then.'

Within these few days, Mehr had come to know a great deal about the guerrillas. All that she had heard was almost of a kind. Somewhere, beyond the borders, they were undergoing military training. They attacked the Pakistani soldiers at night. They collected arms and ammunition in this way. The Khan soldiers were angry. They had attacked the guerrilla camps across the river by helicopter a while ago. Nobody could say what the losses were. Now they were coming by boat, since it was difficult to come by land during the rainy season.

It seemed as though a gramophone record was playing inside the lady's mouth. Mehr realized that Islampur was not any ordinary village. It was a regular guerrilla camp. But only the men were fighting. The women were silent spectators. They cooked, fed, sent the soldiers out to battle, but could do nothing themselves. That was the custom, the tradition. It was because of this tradition that they were helpless.

The lady whispered, 'I know where the men have gone. Nobody else in the village knows.'

This time Mehr could not control her curiosity. She asked, 'Where?'

She replied, 'To attack the ship.'

'Where?'

'I don't know where the ship is. It's come from the direction of Rongpur,' she replied.

Mehr felt uncomfortable. It was becoming unbearable. Why were women so helpless? A war of liberation was going on. And the women were just cooking in their homes. They were objects of lust for the Khans. They were mere spectators, victims of the worst exploitation, of molestation.

The older wife was neglected in this house. But both her sons had joined the Mukti Bahini. They had been in Hindustan earlier. None in this house knew the whereabouts of the boys at this point of time. They did not even know if they were dead or alive. She had no opportunity to ask anybody. Her husband had no time these days.

And the little time when he was at home, he spent with his younger wife. For the younger wife was the favoured one. She was still in the full bloom of her youth.

The older wife bore her husband's neglect silently. That, too, was the custom, the tradition. Sometimes, she scolded the younger wife; at others, she blamed fate. Within a few hours of her arrival, Mehr knew all the ins and outs of this household. The older wife was abandoned. But she would have to suffer this rejection in silence. For it was not a sin for a man to marry and have two or three wives. But the rules for women were different. Of course, it was men who made the laws for women.

The rains continued without any let-up.

The senior wife called both of them for dinner. She, too, sat down for the meal. The three of them began to talk as they ate in the kitchen.

The senior wife had listened attentively to whatever Mehr had said ever since she had arrived here. She had asked about her background, where she was from and about her family. Listening to her story, the older woman lamented, 'Muslims are killing Muslims. Muslim men are dishonouring Muslim women. Khoda will never tolerate this.'

Mehr paused at her meal. She stared at the elder wife. After a few moments, she said, addressing her as 'elder mother', 'Look, Borma. How can you say that the Khans are Muslims? They are no longer Muslims. That's what the mullahs are saying. They are with us, the mullahs.'

The senior wife said with astonishment, 'Let your words come to be, my dear . . .' She paused. 'I don't understand any of this at all. All the Muslims got together and chased away the Hindus to create Pakistan. But rivers of blood have flowed in Pakistan. A cracked bamboo cannot be joined again. My two boys have gone. My husband has left home for battle. It's not just in this one house. It's the same story in almost every house.'

The younger wife looked at the older one's face and said, 'They have done the right thing.'

Mehr was surprised. She asked the younger woman, addressing her as an elder brother's wife, 'Bou, aren't you afraid? If something were to happen to Roushana's father . . .'

The younger wife replied without any hesitation, 'If he dies, he dies. What's the point of being afraid? The way things are going these days, women, too, will have to fight.'

'It's not good to be so aggressive, Najma, don't brag,' said the older woman. 'Do women ever fight?'

'Since the men aren't able to succeed on their own, why will the women remain sitting? Those Khans will burn down our houses, kill the babies on our laps and dishonour us. Are we supposed to just stare at them with eyes wide open? I'll kill at least one, before I die myself.' Najma spoke in an agitated voice.

To prevent the argument from escalating further, Mehr asked, 'Will you be able to do that?'

Najma swallowed a large quantity of rice before replying, 'Of course I will. I shall not let them have my body, like the others.'

Mehr said nothing. After finishing their meal, all three of them washed the utensils and put them away. Popping betel nuts in their mouth, they latched the doors and went inside the huge mosquito net. Soon the older lady fell asleep.

But Mehr could not. She lay awake and talked late into the night with Najma. She, too, spoke of her troubles and sorrows. Najma talked about her preparations. She had taken a decision. Even her husband did not know of this. If there was trouble, she would take her husband's sharp spear and confront them.

Mehr wanted to laugh. That spear would be of no use at all. But she kept quiet. After a while, both of them fell asleep.

6

When she awoke the next day, Najma was not there on the bamboo mat. Neither was her daughter or the older wife. A ray of sunlight had entered through a chink in the wall. It had come through the mosquito net to rest on her face. She lay on the mat for a while, before finally getting up.

The older wife was cooking. Najma had had a bath and was changing her clothes. The little girl was playing with a kid in the courtyard. Seeing her, Najma said, 'Go and have your bath. We shall have to go to the fields.'

Without replying, Mehr silently went to the pond. After her bath, she loosened her hair in the golden sunshine and looked up. The sky was clear today. She offered her namaz. It was as though a nightmare had come to an end. Ever since she had left her own village, she had spent her days and nights with the guerrillas. They were without boundaries. They lived unconfined, like the homeless bauls, the singing minstrels, who roamed the land. Countless youth had left their homes. Without a home, though, women felt so helpless!

Even if it was somebody else's, this was, after all, a house. A home. The pond was calm. On its edges stood tamarind, jolphai, areca nut, betel nut and other plants. All was quiet and peaceful. On the other side were the fields, now brimming over with water. Jute was thriving in those fields. She stood staring at that scene for a long time. Filled with a sense of boundless peace, she returned to the house. It was getting late.

Najma and the others had, in the meantime, had their meal and were ready to leave. Looking towards Mehr, Najma smiled and said, 'We are going to the fields. We have to plant rice seedlings. You stay and guard the house. I have served your food. It's right there . . .'

Najma tied her infant on her back and came and stood near Mehr. She noticed Najma's beauty. A sweet fragrance, like that of the bokul bloom, came from her. Mehr felt very close to Najma. 'When will you be back?' she asked.

'It will be late. Roushana's father will not be coming back today either. Will you be scared?'

Najma's tone was sweetly teasing. The older wife had already left.

Mehr asked, 'What if he returns?' She had met Najma's husband briefly when she had arrived here, but he had left shortly after.

Najma laughed out loud. 'You are more worried than I am!' Mehr blushed with embarrassment. Najma continued, 'There's no problem, even if he returns. He will not bother you.'

Mehr had to laugh at this.

Najma left with the baby. The cattle and goats, chicken and ducks were all out of their pens. After eating, Mehr washed up the utensils and came out to the courtyard. From the end of the pathway, she looked at the village. The place was quiet. Only the voices of a few old men could be heard nearby. In the distance the river gleamed faintly. At that very point the river took a sharp bend. She turned back, closed the door and lay down to sleep.

She did not know how long she had slept. She woke up, suddenly, to the roar of machine gun fire. It was like thunder without a break.

She went outside. In the distance, flames leapt up to the sky. Mehr realized what was happening. She returned to the house. She heard a voice inside her, urging, 'Run! Run away!'

Mehr picked up the revolver. She latched the front door and went out by the back gate. Beyond the yard, behind the house, were the jute fields and the jungles. The unknown friend within her advised her to hide there. Slowly, she went and concealed herself in the forest. She kept a watch on the house from her hiding place.

Some bullets landed in Najma's house, too. People were running all around, helter-skelter. Old and young, men and women were all running towards where she was hiding. They entered the forest. But nobody came up to where she was. She looked all around intently. But it was not enough. She would have to have a thousand eyes in order to find out what they were doing and where they were going.

The Khan soldiers had surrounded the village and were pressing forward, destroying everything in their path. Houses, barns, sheds—everything blazed fiercely. They seized whatever cattle, goats, chicken and raw provisions they came across and took them towards the landing on the river.

Suddenly, two old men from the village came and stood beside her. They did not see her. One of them said, 'All misfortune comes from the enemy within the house. There is no escape. They are chasing us from all directions.' The man was gasping.

The other old man replied, 'Abdul Matin's people have sent for them . . .'

Suddenly, both of them began running towards the marshy land. Perhaps they had seen the soldiers approaching the place where they were standing. Cautiously, she crept into thicker forest. The bullets began to rain relentlessly all around her on the marshes and forests. She could hear the screams of men, women and children. There were flames all around.

A few soldiers came to where the old men had been standing. They looked all around. A villager pointed to the spot where she was.

No doubt he knew that she was there.

The man slashed away the undergrowth and bushes with a machete. Her hiding place gone, a Khan soldier noticed her immediately. The man who accompanied him, the person who had cut the bushes, said, 'I was right, Sahab. She is a guerrilla.'

Mehr readied herself, revolver in hand.

He looked at her, and said, 'It's no use hiding now. Come out.' He came forward towards her. There was no other way out of this difficulty. She aimed the revolver at his chest and fired. The man stopped. Mehr trembled. The torture inflicted on her Xoruma flashed in her mind. She saw the two Khan soldiers talk excitedly. Najma's words came to her mind. 'I shall not let them have my body, like the others.'

The deity within her said, 'It's no use firing at the soldiers. Kill yourself.'

She made her decision. She remembered Habib. What would he think? Surely he would not mind. It was much better to die than to let the Khan soldiers touch her. She offered namaz in her mind. She then cried out, 'Allah, Allah', and closing her eyes, shot at herself.

The two Khan soldiers were caught unawares. She slumped to the ground.

7

When she regained consciousness, Mehr realized that there was a large bandage on the right side of her chest. She was lying on a bed in a small cabin. She looked around. The door of the cabin was open. She saw that it was raining incessasantly. She saw a vast, swift-flowing river too. A few small boats plied on its waters. The boatmen were taking their boats in the opposite direction to that of the ship. They were absorbed in their task. The ship was moving very slowly, perhaps towards the north. Mehr had not yet regained her sense of direction.

The ship came to the shallower waters near the bank of the river. She saw hazily the familiar and charming picture of the rural landscape with its mango, jamun, jackfruit and betel trees. The little huts seemed to peep at her and beckon in various ways as gracefully as the Baul dancers, saying, 'Come, come, come!'

Suddenly, a Gaji song that she had heard during the fairs of the Nilpuja of the spring month of Sot, and the Durga Puja of the autumn, came to her mind.

Jamdoot Kaaldoot Dainey Aar Baye . . .
The Messenger of Death, the Herald of Time,

Sit to the right, and to the left,
With them sits, in the centre, the Lord of Death.

By invoking his name.
The virtues of the saint Gaji,
Chase away the messengers of Death.

They seemed to be pictures from hell. Death, and Death's messengers were all over her entire body, left and right, on her head and her back. Through the physical agony, along with the vignettes of the village, she saw the carpet of light-blue flowers which bloomed, unconcerned, in the middle of the marshes. She also saw, hidden in the bamboo groves, the weeping pond of red lotuses like the evening sunlight on the swift-flowing currents of the Jamuna, a helpless mother holding the crimson blooms to her breast, weeping heartrendingly. Unconsciously, her own heart wailed in despair. She remembered her village, now burned down and totally destroyed, and sighed. In her mind's eyes, she saw alert tiya birds on the huge banyan trees staring ahead with an unblinking gaze. She heard the cawing of crows and saw the herons standing on one leg each on the marshy banks, the masroka and uk birds searching for food, the fishermen with their nets in the middle of the river, the now-closed school building, the huge, dense forest which sometimes showed itself. With the sudden calls of unknown birds, the quiet forest would come to life. Her eyes grew moist. She thought that she was in the Boitoroni river at the entrance to the kingdom of Jomraja, the lord of death.

She could not understand what was happening. She had aimed her gun at her breast. By now, vultures and jackals should have finished off her body as it lay in the undergrowth of the forest beside the jute fields. After all, so many had ended up like that. How had she survived, who had brought her to this ship, who had bandaged her, who had nursed her, who had brought her to life in this dead land and forced her to remain alive like a spirit? Unable to understand a thing, she began to recall in her mind the events leading up to her death and began to study the gaps in them. But she could comprehend nothing. There was no solution to this mystery. Tears streamed down from her eyes.

At that point, she noticed the drizzly world outside. It was afternoon. She heard the melody of somebody singing on the ship. She grew even more confused. Her heart filled with sadness. She recognized a few lines of the song. It seemed to be an Agomoni Geet, welcoming Goddess Durga on her annual visit to earth. Autumn heralded the coming of Durga Puja. Young women, living in the joint families of their marital homes, suffering all kinds of cruelties in the hands of their mothers-in-law, would soon travel back on boats to their natal homes. Their mothers, happy in their expectation, would wait restlessly for their arrival. Their hearts would weep for the daughters who had been married off in a distant land. So many boats sailed between the two villages, yet there was no sign of their girls. The mother's heart keeps wondering which boat would bring her daughter. But she does not come. Tears flow from the mother's eyes. Who will wipe away those tears?

Gulam Moula, who will wipe away my tears,
In which boat will my Gauri arrive,
So many boats come and go . . .

Mehr was now totally heartbroken. Would she ever be able to go back to her mother's bosom? Xoruma was in her watery grave in the pond. Babajan was lost in the huge blaze that had consumed their home. There was no news of her friend Malobika. Habib, Sameer, Ismail and the others were locked in mortal combat. And what about Najma?

True, she had come to Jom's city, the abode of the god of death. But perhaps Fate had decreed that there were still some years left to her. Perhaps this was why Death's henchmen had kept her in captivity. What would they do to her after this? She became afraid. Would there be a repeat of all that was happening in the entire land of Bangladesh yet again? She was too weak to even jump into the river and die, if this were to happen. She could not get up from her bed at all.

Gradually, the grass on the bank of the river went out of sight. The rain continued incessantly. From afar came the sorrowful sound of a cricket and the frightening howls of jackals. Her entire body was wracked with pain. The wind grew stronger, even as the darkness deepened.

Suddenly, somebody entered the cabin, closed the door and switched on the light. She saw a handsome, bright-eyed, well built, fair young man in a military uniform. She looked sharply at him. She seemed to recollect that she had seen him somewhere before. She realized that he was one of the Khan soldiers that she had seen in the forest behind Najma's house in Islampur in the moments before her suicide bid. Her face and eyes expressed her fear and anger. By now, she was in no doubt that she was a prisoner of the Khans. She felt quite helpless. She began to take Allah's name silently.

The man was very tall. His hands were fair, his fingers sturdy. Putting his hand on her forehead to check if she had fever, he asked slowly in broken Bangla, 'How long have you been conscious?'

Mehr did not answer. She did not feel like replying.

The man paused. He then examined her entire body as though the Almighty had made some grave mistake in creating her form. But there was no lust, sympathy, or kindness in it. There was no cruelty either. It was a detached look.

He paused. Smiling, he took out a revolver from his pocket and then asked dramatically, 'Do you recognize this?'

She was annoyed. She replied, 'Yes, I recognize it. When will you kill me? Will you kill me with my own revolver? Are you trying to tell me that?'

'No,' he replied. 'Actually, I want to tell you something. Even though you are a guerrilla, you were not trained to use a revolver properly. The man you shot at did not die. Neither did you. The bullet did not hit the proper spot.' He paused and then added, 'If you don't believe me, I can call the man and show you. Do you want to see him?'

'No. What's the point of that?' she asked indifferently.

The man's face saddened. Perhaps he had thought that because he had saved her, her face and eyes would soften with gratitude. He put the revolver back into his pocket and said, 'When I heard Allah's name on your lips, I immediately changed my mind. I did not shoot you. Allah saved you. We may be Punjabis, but we are Muslims.'

Mehr did not reply. She examined the man's face seriously. Allah surely exists, she thought. Otherwise, why would this butcher's stone heart soften? Why would he show kindness? She believed that Allah had saved her. This belief gave her strength. She asked abruptly, 'If you are Muslims, why are you killing us? What harm have we done to you?'

The man replied, 'You do not know anything about the rules of politics and military takeovers. That's why you can ask this question so innocently.' His face hardened abruptly. 'Khoda will certainly not punish those who kill the people who wish to divide Pakistan into two pieces. This is Jihad.'

Mehr recollected some words from the Quran. She had read those lines in Yakub's diary. Zubeida had written those lines and sent them to him. 'Those who believe in Allah, those who follow the path of belief in the unquestioned supremacy of Allah as the One, fight in His Name. And those who do not believe in the unquestioned supremacy of Allah as the One are on the side of Shaitan. Those who commit injustices are friends of Shaitan. Fight therefore against the friends of Satan. In reality, Satan's side is not strong.' She began to murmur those lines to herself.

The man smiled and said, 'I have found both Yakub's diary and Zubeida's photo inside your blouse. That's the second reason for saving you. I knew Yakub. We are from the same place, though our regiments are different. Where did you meet Yakub?'

'In Kalihati,' replied Mehr. 'Our village.'

The man seemed to wish to find out about the whole incident. He had heard about Yakub's death. Mehr saw a great curiosity on his face. He wished to find out more, about how, where, and in what condition Yakub had died. Why was there such emotion for his friend? Yakub had inhumanly killed the helpless villagers as though they were cattle. She pictured that stone-hearted butcher again. But strangely, the fire of hatred and terror in her mind was gradually dying down. In the desert of the man's cruel heart, somewhere, Allah had hidden the water of Phorat.

She remembered those horrific incidents that had happened in Malobika's home in Kalihati. Slowly, she recounted those incidents. She did not leave out a single occurrence, a single scene. It did not even occur to her that she should hide anything regarding Habib and Siddiqui. She wished only to relate the truth as it was. Pure and simple. From the time she had been hiding and quietly witnessing the battle to where she had said the last prayers for her Xoruma as her body lay in the pond, and later, when, after meeting Siddiqui, she came to meet up with the group of guerrillas. She left out nothing in her straightforward narration of events.

The description took some time. She noticed the grief in the man's face as she finished her narration. He questioned, 'So he asked you for water?'

'Yes,' Mehr replied. 'After drinking the water, he looked at me with gratitude. Silently, without complaining about his pain, he just closed his eyes. There was no time for me to even look at where he had been wounded. I did not even weep, even after seeing Malobika in that condition. The Khan soldiers are butchers. They are enemies of women.'

Mehr grew agitated. Without her being aware of it, her eyes grew damp. It wasn't as though Yakub's death had not created an impression in her mind. It had. She got the feeling that the soldier before her, who had questioned her with sensitivity, wished to say something, but could not.

'Is there anything else you want to know?' she asked.

He paused, then asked with great difficulty, 'Do you think Yakub did something like that? I mean . . .'

Mehr responded without hesitation, 'No. Perhaps, Yakub was a good man.'

The man replied, 'Yes. He was good.' After a brief pause, he said again, 'I too have not done anything like that. Believe me. I have a wife and a sister at home. Zubeida is also a distant cousin of mine. I am doing my duty. The Bengalis here are rebelling against Pakistan. The general has given orders to quell the rebellion. Certainly, I have killed. But I have not done anything of that kind.'

She could not understand why this soldier had to say all this to her. She could, therefore, not restrain herself from commenting, 'Nobody will believe you in this land today. Everybody believes all of you to be Shaitan. Satan himself.'

'What do you think?'

'I think the same. What difference does it make if there are one or two considerate men here and there if almost the entire army is like that?' she said.

The man's face turned grave. 'The same thing looks different when looked at from the other side. You are trying to break Pakistan into pieces.' He paused. 'Pakistan has to be saved.'

'Has Allah told us to commit atrocities in the Quran?'

The man did not reply. After quite some time, he said, 'I just want to know one more thing. Nobody wants us here. Why?'

Mehr remained silent for a moment. She then said, 'I cannot answer such a big question. Sheikh Mujibur will be able to do so. But I remember some words from the Quran. In the Quran, Allah has said that if somebody behaves in a wicked and immoral way with you, then respond by behaving in a virtuous and moral way with him. If you had done that, surely you would not have been hated so much here. I do not know about faults, about errors. But what harm have my Xoruma, Malobika, or I done? What have the villagers done to you? You have weapons. Why have you raised these weapons against the weak, the helpless? You have made me a destitute, helpless. What crime have I committed?'

The man said sharply, 'But you joined the guerrillas.'

Mehr replied, 'I am not a guerrilla. I would possibly have felt better if I could have joined the guerrillas.'

The man laughed. It was a simple uncomplicated laugh. He said, 'We are investigating.'

'What are you investigating?' Mehr asked, agitated.

He smiled. Instead of responding in a straightforward manner, he asked, 'So, are you in love with Habib?'

Mehr responded simply, 'Even if I am, why do you ask?'

He examined Mehr's face minutely. It was the colour of ripe paddy. He said, 'Perhaps we can forgive you if you can make Habib stop what he is doing and leave. Habib has harmed us the most in this area. He will surely listen to you since you love him.'

Mehr thought over the man's words for a long time. She then replied, 'I do not have that power. He loves the country more than he loves me.' She remained silent after that.

The man did not answer. He suddenly noticed that Mehr's entire body was shivering. Placing his palm on her forehead, he said, 'Your fever is probably rising. Go to sleep. We shall talk some more tomorrow. I am truly grateful to you for giving water to Yakub in his dying moments and slaking his thirst. You will be comfortable as long as you are here with me. But I do not know what will happen later. I, too, am a prisoner of rules. An obedient soldier. You may even be brought to trial later.'

'There's no need for any trial,' she said. 'If you are my well-wisher, just kill me. Or else, just let me die.'

Looking into her eyes, the man said affectionately, 'Don't worry so much. Don't keep thinking about dying. I shall do whatever you wish.'

Opening the door, the man left, closing it again after himself.

Mehr had a high fever. But even in the middle of her pain, her anguish, she came to believe that Khoda existed. Khoda's mercy, too, existed.

8

She had a high temperature for three days. In her feverish condition, she felt dizzy, even while in bed. When the scenes of the terrible tortures came to her mind, she felt a sense of helplessness. When she thought of her own captivity, an unknown dread pierced through her mind. She would lose faith even in Khoda. She would scream, 'Allah! I have nobody!'

The man would come in every afternoon and evening. He checked her fever, gave her medication, fed her food meant for convalescents, spoke of Yakub and asked about the guerrilla bands. She realized that he knew a great deal about medical care. He even talked of his life in Lahore one day. He had never thought that he would join the armed forces. Neither had Yakub. He had studied medicine. Yakub had joined college and dreamt of becoming a lawyer and joining politics. They were very much against military rule. Some, like Bhutto, Wali Khan and others had been agitating to get rid of the military rulers. He supported that movement wholeheartedly.

In the meantime, though, the influence of the Awami League grew stronger in East Pakistan. Yahya Khan had not yet come to power at that time. There was a strong rumour all around the land that East Pakistan had joined hands with India and rebelled.

There was a blood relationship as well as economic ties between his family and that of Yakub's. There had been inter-marriage between both the families, though admittedly it was a distant relationship. His father had married a girl from Yakub's family. She was of the same lineage and belonged to a respected land-owning family. She had got quite a lot of property. Yakub's father worked in a bank and held an important position. They were Kathiawari Memons and had fled Bombay during Partition. And he was from the lineage of Khoja Sheikh.

The people of both communities were of respected ancestry. However, the families were not all uniformly wealthy. Even though both their families were not as powerful compared to the others, they had riches as well as pride of ancestry. The mill, banking and some other businesses of Pakistan were in the hands of the Memons and Khoja Sheikh families. They were the kingmakers. They moved around and dined with ministers, presidents, governors, officers, merchants and powerful foreigners. There was a lot of social interaction among them, a lot of give and take. Iskandar Mirza, Ayub Khan, Yahya Khan–none of them could do without the support and goodwill of these two families. When Sheikh Mujibur's Awami League began their agitation for full autonomy, the heads of both the families were infuriated.

Meanwhile, Ayub Khan had brought in arms and ammunition, economic aid, machinery, tanks and machine guns from the United States and was building up his armed forces. He needed good officers. He searched high and low for young, energetic, vigorous men. There was a great deal of tumult in schools and colleges. The elders of the Memon and Sheikh Khoja families applauded Ayub Khan. The media–newspapers and the radio–made much of this tumult and gave it extensive coverage.

One day, there came the news that China had invaded India and defeated the Indian soldiers. Their fathers were overjoyed that day.

They made preparations to liberate Kashmir. Ayub Khan, backed by his friendship with China, created such an atmosphere of triumph that it seemed as though Pakistan had seized a glorious victory from all sides while India was on the verge of being vanquished. The destruction of Sheikh Mujibur seemed imminent.

There was a huge requirement for good soldiers. Young men were in urgent demand. Ayub had fulfilled all other needs and was held in high esteem. The rebels had to be taught a lesson and the patriots wanted more power.

Enough. The call went out to hostels, fields, homes, villages and cities. Thousands upon thousands of young men came forward to save Islam and Pakistan. How could the youths of the Memon clan remain unmoved by this call of the Holy War? He and Yakub and he enrolled in the armed forces on the same day.

This happened five years ago. After their training, they were posted for a while in Lahore. When war with India broke out in 1965, there were cries of victory all around. It was likely that this time it would be very easy to march in and occupy Delhi in their Patton tanks. As for Kashmir, it would be a pushover. On the Lahore front, there were battles between Patton and Vaijayanta tanks. There were massive battles in the skies between Sabre jets and Gnats. They dreamed of annexing Kashmir and taking over Delhi. If China gave them a little help and if Indian soldiers could be kept busy fighting in the northern borders, perhaps, then, the Pakistani Army could go directly to East Pakistan through Delhi, via a corridor that they would create. At last, the Quaid-e-Azam's dream would come true.

But none of this happened. They went forth like eagles, but returned crestfallen, like owls, to the heart of Lahore. The people of the Sheikh Khoja and Memon clans had to flee for their lives to Karachi. Lahore was certainly dark at night, but it began to seem shadowy even during the day. Patton tanks, Sabre jets, the cannons of the United States and China all fell silent. Ayub Sahab lost face before the nations of the world. Later, the Tashkent Accord was signed. Lal Bahadur Shastri took pity and the Soviet Union also put pressure. The Indian forces withdrew on their own accord from the banks of the Ichhogil canal back to their original pre-war position.

It was at that time that he and Yakub and he came to know Habib. He was then a havildar, a constable, in the East Pakistan Rifles. That was the first time that either of them had seen a soldier from East Pakistan. They were under the impression that they were thin, dark and puny. They had heard from their fathers and grandfathers that the Bengalis were not human, that they were Lilliputs. Dwarves. Ten Bangla soldiers were needed to defeat a single Khan soldier. They had tiny hearts which thudded fearfully at the very sight of a gun. They did not have the ability to work hard. Leave alone defending their own country, they were not even able to run their own offices, factories, industries or businesses. Punjabis and Sindhis had to do everything for them. All that they liked to do was to gather unnecessarily and chatter uselessly or to sing.

But the two of them realized their mistake when they saw Habib and his friends fighting. When the Indian Vaijayanta tanks came valiantly forward towards the Ichhogil canal, their own regiment from West Pakistan did not have the courage to counter them. But the Bengalis decided in a moment that they would form 'suicide squads' and march on ahead. They did it, too. But they could not stop the Indian forces from their forward march.

That self-sacrifice had an important consequence. The Pakistani forces regained their self-confidence. Hope returned to their minds in a flood like the rising tide of the sea. But the war ended at that point.

Habib was the leader of a suicide squad. Nobody knew how he survived that journey. He had destroyed a Vaijayanta tank on his own. The soldiers of the other side had no doubt fired. The bullets had not pierced his heart. As in the case of Mehr, it had gone past the ribs on the right side of his chest. He had fled in that condition.

Later, he had been rescued by a helicopter. After the war had ended, both Yakub and he had gone to the hospital in Lahore Cantonment to see Habib. He had talked with them just like Mehr had. Even though he was Bengali, Habib was fair complexioned, well built and with a ready smile.

It was then that they had, for the first time, heard about East Pakistan and the Bengalis. Their language, literature, rivers, jute, paddy, sugarcane, melons, mustard, tobacco, cotton, tea, bamboo—they had an abundance of everything. They sang songs, laughed, toiled throughout the day and then rested in their huts in the evenings. They battled floods and hurricanes. Diving into the water, they reaped jute with their knives. The snakes and the tigers from the Sundarbans floated on the water, swimming alongside the river with dolphins and ghariyals, of the rivers Padma-Jamuna-Brahmaputra. In their spare time, they took part in jatras, theatres, music and dance and enjoyed themselves . . . Every year, they observed Eid and Muharram. They would consistently, every morning and evening, give the call to prayer in their mosques. Prayers were offered regularly. Nikahs, weddings, took place often. Boats would ply on the waves of the vast rivers. All kinds of commodities were ferried on those boats and small businesses conducted. Jute, cotton, mustard, paddy and so much else! But they themselves did not get the proper price for any of those commodities.

There were beautiful pleasure boats with colourful sails that plied on the river. People would go for long leisure trips on these. The boatmen would sing their Bhatiali songs as they poled their boats onwards. There were trains and ships too. Nowadays, there were airplanes too, to go to places in the interior. Hindus, Muslims and Christians all lived together there.

However, people were not completely happy. All their hard work came to nothing. The best jobs went to the people of West Pakistan. Even in the armed forces, their own people were in the lower rungs. And yet the majority of Pakistanis lived in the eastern side. On the other hand, the prices of all essentials were sky high. The greater part of the paddy crop was harvested there. The land yielded golden harvests. And yet the people had to buy rice at fifty to sixty rupees per maund.

'What?' Yakub had asked Habib with surprise. 'But in Lahore, the price of rice is twenty five rupees!'

Habib had smiled crookedly. It was a mocking, sarcastic smile. He had said that it wasn't just rice, everything else was much more expensive in the East. For the first time, the two of them came to know that mustard oil, which sold for one rupee per seer in Lahore, was five times more expensive in East Pakistan. Five rupees. Wheat was fifteen rupees a maund in Lahore. In East Pakistan, the monopolistic merchants sold it for thirty rupees a maund. Gold was 135 rupees in the Karachi market. In Dhaka it was 170 rupees. Yakub was a student of economics. He was astonished. Later, he told Habib, 'None of us here know the real truth. Things seem to be in a huge mess there.'

Habib was in Lahore for four months. During that time, they did much more than just talk with him. They spent their time in all kinds of activities. They swam and played together, especially hockey, a game in which Habib excelled. They had had no idea that Bengalis could play hockey so well. They ate together, went for movies and sang together. He sang Bhatialis and Ghazals beautifully. They would go to Zubeida's home and eat grapes, kishmish, fruits and much else. Habib became their intimate friend.

They felt sad when Habib went back. But what did it matter whether a soldier felt good or bad, happy or sad?

One day, Yakub was transferred to another regiment. Lutfur himself was brought to Karachi. A few years went by quite well. But abruptly, Ayub Khan passed on the reins of government to the powerful Pathan Yahya Khan to lead a quiet, retired life at his home.

As one Shahenshah's fate waned, another's waxed strong. They then realized that the man was not at all that they had thought him to be. Even the moon had a blot on her face. They heard that he had amassed a huge fortune through corrupt means. Bhutto Saheb alleged that Ayub had gifted Kashmir to India at Tashkent. They also heard that by letting the language agitation grow stronger, Ayub Khan was at the root of establishing Mujibur as the hero of the rebels of East Pakistan. Yahya Khan was now in power. He would not commit the mistakes that Ayub had. Bhutto Saheb began to roar like a tiger. He said that Kashmir would have to be regained. If necessary, they would fight against India for a thousand years.

In due course, Lutfur went home on leave. A bride had been arranged for him. There were celebrations during his nikah with a girl from a wealthy family. Yakub was present on the day of his nikah. He had become very thin. He had been fed like a prince at the wedding. His grandfather and uncles had discussed politics avidly. His father had joined Bhutto Sahab's party. However, most of the people of the family were on the side of Maulana Moududi. The discussions turned to Yahya Khan. He would be holding elections in Pakistan quite soon. Democracy would be established once more. His father said that it would be difficult to finish off the Awami League. If Sheikh Mujibur could not be defeated, Pakistan would be finished.

Yakub had not joined in the conversation. Sitting in a corner, he had listened silently to all that was being said. At one point, Lutfur had called Yakub outside. They went and sat on the back verandah and began to talk. The weak afternoon sunlight was dimming.

'The old men have no sense of what's right or what should be done,' Yakub had said.

'Why?' Lutfur had asked, surprised.

Yakub was fed up. Even if the Prophet himself came, Sheikh Mujibur could not be defeated. Of course the Prophet would be on the side of truth.

'On which side is truth?'

'Do you have to ask that? All this time, the old men have been deceiving us. In the proposal put forward by the Muslim League in 1940 it was said that all regions in Pakistan would get equal representation. Pakistan would be a nation.'

Lutfur had said, 'Without a strong government at the centre, Pakistan will break up into many pieces.'

Yakub was even more irritated. He said, 'Look here, Lutfur. I am not saying this casually. I have studied this. Nobody can keep the Bengalis from rising. They cannot be given independence. But they can surely be given what Mujibur wants. We shall be able to live together if we do so. Otherwise, Pakistan will break into two.'

He had remained quiet. The feasting ended as did his leave. He returned to Karachi. Yakub went to Layalpur. They did not meet for a long time since both lived far away from each other.

There was a general election in the entire country. In East Pakistan, Sheikh Mujibur's party won. Bhutto Sahab and Wali Khan won in West Pakistan. Everything turned topsy-turvy. There was never much talk of politics in the barracks. But they got to know everything from the radio.

One day, Pakistan Radio announced that Yahya Khan had gone to Dhaka. Later, Bhutto Sahab himself followed. In his mind, Yakub prayed to Allah for some solution. But no such thing happened. Both Bhutto Sahab and Yahya Khan returned without anything being resolved.

And after that was heard Yahya Khan's roar like a lion's. Sheikh Mujibur was a traitor. The Awami League was an enemy. India was creating all kinds of conspiracies. What had happened? They could make out nothing. Even as they tried to add up two and two together, they suddenly heard that the head of the armed forces had sent out a strict order. They would have to leave for East Pakistan within twenty four hours.

On enquiry, he found out that Sheikh Mujibur had been imprisoned. The Awami League of East Pakistan was banned. The armed forces were being engaged to crush the rebels. The military had the responsibility of saving Pakistan. He had been posted at

Karachi only to train the Ansar Bahini. It was time for him wrap that up and move to East Pakistan.

Lutfur was not in the military uniform when he alighted at Dhaka airport. The government of Ceylon had stopped the transit of troops through their country. Earlier, flights to East Pakistan could overfly the Indian territory. The Indian government put a stop to that. For the first time, it was felt that East Pakistan was really far away. Sabre jets could not fly directly to Dhaka. They had to stop for refuelling somewhere in between. The route was two thousand kilometres long.

When he landed at Dhaka he saw that it was teeming with soldiers. They kept alighting from aircraft. From that crowd, somebody came and placed a hand on his shoulder and said, 'Lutfur.'

Turning around, he saw that it was Yakub. He looked even gaunter than before. There was a wooden smile on his face. It was actually a sign of sorrow.

'When did you come?' asked Lutfur.

'It's been a month.' Yakub led him away from the runway and said, 'This is the end of Pakistan.'

'What's happened?' he asked. There was amazement on his face and eyes.

'I've been in Dhaka since the 24th. I saw Yahya Khan and Bhutto Sahab on the 25th at the airport. They were going back.' The smile dried up on his lips. In a quiet voice, he said, 'Now that you are here, you will see for yourself.'

'Where have you been put on duty?' asked Lutfur.

'At the airport. Maybe that's the reason that I still remain human. The general mocked me, saying I was a girl. As though they themselves have been behaving like real men.' After a pause, Yakub added, 'I shall have to go to Faridpur today.'

'Why don't you tell me what's happened?' asked Lutfur. 'How is the rebellion faring?'

'Rebellion!' There was sarcasm in Yakub's voice. 'It's not rebellion. It's murder. Genocide. It's arson. It's the rape of women. Nobody has been able to escape the tank and machine gun firing. In the history of a race, it takes the prayers, entreaties and efforts of hundreds of years for a poet, a philosopher, a writer to be born. A single bullet from us finishes them. If this is not the end of Pakistan, what is it?'

Suddenly, somebody called out to Lutfur. He was ordered to move on. Bidding farewell to Yakub, he left, perturbed. They had not met since then. After Faridpur, Yakub had probably been posted in various other places for the next few months. Finally, he had reached Kalihati and breathed his last.

'Tell me, what did he look like at the time of his death?' Lutfur asked Mehr.

Mehr brought to mind Yakub's pale, colourless, thin face. It had been without individuality for her. She replied, 'Not like you. He looked more like a lean Bengali man. I only saw him briefly.' She paused and then added, 'His voice was very sweet.'

Lutfur did not reply. He became quiet.

Mehr asked, 'Is it true or not . . . what Yakub said?'

After a while, Lutfur swallowed and said, 'It's true. But there was no way out. Without doing this, Pakistan could not be saved.'

Mehr grew agitated. Gathering up all her courage, she said, 'Pakistan will not last.'

It was now Lutfur who became agitated. He put his hand on the revolver in his pocket, then stopped. He said, 'Mehr. Don't say that. I am a soldier. A pure Punjabi soldier. I have eaten the salt of Pakistan. I shall be loyal to the salt of Pakistan. If some other Bengali had said this, I would have shot him dead immediately.'

Instead of being cowed down, Mehr said, 'I shall be so happy to die. Everybody else—all my relatives—are dead. Why should I alone remain alive? Besides, this body has become a burden for me. Kill me, kill me. You've killed many others.'

Lutfur said desolately, 'I cannot kill you.'

'Why?'

He smiled, but did not reply.

A few more days passed in this manner. Gradually, Lutfur stopped talking about Yakub with Mehr. He began to speak about Habib instead.

In the meantime, Mehr had recovered. Blood had returned to her face.

The ship continued its journey till it reached Gowalondo. It remained docked there for two full days. Not once, in those two days, did Mehr meet Lutfur. During that time, she tried to go out several times from her cabin to see the town of Gowalondo from the ship. But a sentry at the door did not allow her to come out. It was the captain's orders, it seemed. It was not possible to see the town properly through the side on which the door opened. She remained confined.

She was a prisoner.

After two days, the ship began its return journey. In these two days, she had come to know from the khansamah, the cook, who brought her meals, that there was not just this one ship. There were several others together moving in a fleet.

'What news of the captain?' she asked.

The khansamah was in a singlet and shorts. He had come to give her lunch. He replied, 'Please have your meal first.'

Mehr looked at the man. There was an expression of deference on his face. She said, 'I will. Tell me, what news of him?'

Hesitatingly, the khansamah said, 'When we were in Gowalondo, he left the ship and went somewhere. He didn't return.'

'What!'

The khansamah said, 'Bibi Sahiba, we've heard that Qader's gang has got him. They captured him in his vehicle.'

Mehr was thunderstruck. Agitated, she asked, 'Is he dead or alive?'

He sighed. 'How can I say, Bibi Sahiba?' he asked.

'Okay. Tell me, where are all these ships going?' asked Mehr. A thought had crossed her mind. She felt uncertain about her own future.

'They are going towards Rongpur, Bibi Sahiba. They are carrying mal masala, stuff,' he replied.

Mehr remained in the dark about what 'mal masala' could mean. She asked, 'Is it arms and ammunition?'

'Yes,' the cook paused and added, 'And . . .' he laughed.

Her body trembled. There was something in his tone that made her shiver. She asked, 'And what?'

'Bibi Sahiba, the Sahibs need all kinds of things. Liquor, women, grapes, khishmish.' He smiled once more as he said this.

When Mehr heard this, she felt as though her entire being had been polluted. He had aimed this at her. She could guess quite easily what this meant. She could make out the mockery that was targeted at the dignity of women. She felt humiliated, ashamed.

The khansamah was an experienced person. He could make out the turmoil and anguish in her mind just by looking at Mehr's eyes. Sighing, he said sympathetically, 'It's only for the sake of my belly that I'm working here, Bibi Sahiba. I've come from a far away. I've seen many people in this condition. Really, what has the world come to! People are killed as though they were chickens. Women are devoured as though they were alcohol. It's all an addiction. I've seen tigers in the Sundarbans. Once it tastes human blood, there's no stopping it. It becomes a man-eater. Mymensingh, Tangail, Pabna, Rongpur, Gabla, Dinajpur—the Sahibs are very angry with the people of these places, Bibi Sahiba. They've not been able to make any inroads into these places. Many soldiers have died.'

The khansamah became silent.

Mehr wanted to hear more. But the cook got ready to leave. He could not be a friend. Even though he sympathized with her, he was only a servant in the Pakistani armed forces. Mehr asked him, 'Is there a new captain on this ship?'

'Yes.'

'Who?'

'Somebody or the other . . . I've forgotten the name, Bibi Sahiba.

But I've seen him once before. He's not a very good person.' The khansamah left.

Mehr's worries intensified. Lutfur had told her that she was safe as long as she was in his care. He did not know what would happen after that. Her future was uncertain. Sitting on her bunk, she looked at the river outside. She was sick and tired of it all. Her mind was riddled with disgust and fear.

There was chicken curry and rice for dinner. She did not even touch the meal. When the khansamah came to clear the dishes, she asked him abruptly, 'Were there other women in this ship before, as well?'

'Bibi Sahiba! It's better not to ask me those things. These people have harems all over.' He paused and then said, 'Why, you haven't eaten a thing!'

'No, I don't feel like eating.'

Mehr looked at the man, and asked, 'Where do you come from?'

'I was originally from Bihar. Now my home is in Dhaka.'

The man laughed, again. He then said, 'You asked about captain, didn't you? This captain's name is Kamaluzzaman.'

Mehr said nothing.

The cook began to clear the table. Mehr glanced occasionally at him and he too looked at her every now and again. Neither of them could muster up the courage to speak openly to the other. They had seen each other these past few days, but there had been no real conversation between them. It had been Lutfur who had filled her mind. There was some barrier between the two of them now. There was a look of helplessness in Mehr's eyes. The khansamah certainly understood this. While leaving, he smiled and said, 'It's not that each and every tiger is a man-eater, Bibi Sahiba. But they are very few. Lutfur Sahab was not a bad man. But not everybody is Lutfur Sahab.'

Gradually, dusk had begun to beat its wings to alight upon this world. The air was sultry, but there was no sign of rain anywhere. She opened the porthole and looked out at the glimmering waters of the confluence of the Padma and Jamuna. There was no agitation anywhere. Gradually, the ghat of Gowalondo, the landing pier, was left behind. It became indistinct. The khansamah's words kept ringing in her ears.

She began to think of her own future.

Once, when she had called out to Allah in supplication, it had touched Lutfur's heart. If she called out once more, then surely it would touch the heart of another oppressor. When Duhsasana had tried to humiliate Draupadi by pulling off her sari to expose her nakedness, Krishna himself had come to her rescue. Was this a fable or the actual truth? She did not know.

She recollected Kamal's face. The tailor Kamal of Kalihati. How hard he had tried to win over her heart. He had stitched beautiful petticoats, blouses, handkerchiefs and tried, in so many ways, to make her understand. Nothing came of it. It was Habib who was in her heart. Habib was educated, well built and a skilled soldier. But he had spurned her as a village girl. He would visit them quite frequently while he was at Jamalpur. He would have all kinds of discussions with Babajan. He would take out time from those discussions to talk with her. Not just when he was working. She had loved Habib since she was a young girl. Habib's home, too, was in Kalihati.

How many nights had she dreamed of getting married to Habib. Even those dreams seemed unreal now. In this virgin's mind today, there were no romantic dreams of a wedding night. Instead, there was an ugly power that threatened her. She did not know the name of that power. All she knew was that it was a demonic power.

9

Mehr did not narrate what happened next. Nor did she say how she got through the next few hours. Perhaps a woman, especially a virgin, can never say these things to a man. But by just looking into her eyes, I could see that her memories terrorized her.

Covering her face with both hands, she said with difficulty, 'The new captain asked me many questions that night. Where were the guerrilla camps? Where was Habib? Which route did Siddiqui and his men take to go to India?' He wanted to know everything about Sameer, Ismail and all the others. At that time I knew practically nothing. But looking at the man's behaviour, I did not divulge even the little that I knew. After that, he began to treat me badly. In the end, the same dreadful thing happened to me, that which has happened to many mothers and daughters of our country.'

Both Bagaitkar and I lowered our heads. Looking at his watch, Bagaitkar said, 'Pulin Babu hasn't come yet. It's almost four o'clock.'

I didn't say anything. At that point, I was in no mind to think of the time. I imagined the ships going over the Jamuna, some demons and a shamed, humiliated, weak, helpless girl. That girl had taken within her the anguish and pain of an entire nation.

The whole country, the entire race, was weeping. We were living in bizarre times. It could not be measured through the hands of the clock. It could only be measured by the victory and defeat of a person's humanity.

The sunlight was fading. Outside, it was becoming gloomy. Suddenly, Mehr said, 'Pulin Babu will come. The poor man has no time. The Mukti Bahini has a lot of problems.' After a pause, she added, 'Listen to the rest of the story. You'll like it.' She resumed her story from where she had left off.

The ship continued its journey. Imprisoned in her cabin, she suffered the torment inflicted on her by the fiend. Daybreak was approaching. Suddenly, she heard a loud scream, the cry of some helpless woman. 'Why have you kept me alive, Allah!'

Who was that woman? So far, she had been under the impression that she was the only woman on board. Who was this other woman? Every now and again, she would scream in anguish. 'Why have you kept me alive, Allah!'

That morning, when the crimson rays of the morning sun gleamed on the waters of the Jamuna, she felt that it was the blood of a woman who had been raped or of a person who had been killed by a bullet or a bayonet. A gentle breeze was coming in through the open porthole, but it brought her no solace. Instead, it brought the fiery flames of chaos and tumult.

The khansamah came, as usual, that day, as well. But there was no smile on his face. He did not even look up at her. Placing the food on the table, he was about to leave in silence.

Suddenly, she said, 'Take it all away. I won't eat anything. I would rather starve to death than eat your food.'

He stopped. 'Why won't you eat, Bibi Sahiba?' he asked.

Mehr replied harshly, 'I'm telling you, take it away.'

'I'm only a servant, Bibi Sahiba. I can't do that.'

He prepared to leave.

Mehr got up and threw the plate with her morning meal and the cup of tea on the floor. The cup shattered, and the tea spilled out. The khansamah exclaimed, 'What have you done! Now the tea will go right out into the veranda!' He began to mop up the tea with the gamosa that was on his shoulder.

The horrifying scream of the woman from the nearby cabin reached her ears. It died down to a ceaseless moaning.

Mehr asked, 'Who is she?'

'She was brought in from the same village as you. Her daughter died.'

'Died?' Mehr asked, agitated.

'How can she not die?' The khansamah stood up, and trembling with anger, he said, 'The new captain is an animal. He snatched the baby from her mother's breast and threw her into the river.'

'Why?' asked Mehr.

'Does an animal reason out anything, Bibi Sahiba? I swear on Kali, I shall run away as soon as I get an opportunity,' said the khansamah.

'What is the woman's name?'

'Najma Bibi.'

'Najma?' Mehr grew numb with shock.

He gathered together the broken pieces and prepared to leave. Abruptly, Mehr asked, 'Will you pass on a message to Najma?'

'What?'

'Tell her that Mehr says Allah exists.' Then, agitatedly, she continued, 'Hey, listen, will you be able to take me to the edge of the railings when the sentry is not around?'

The khansamah looked at Mehr. He said slowly, 'You want to die?'

'Yes. Will you be able to do it?'

The khansamah grew still. After a pause, he asked, 'Why do you want to die?'

'It's better to die than to live like this,' she said.

The khansamah did not say anything. He went out. Not getting a reply, Mehr writhed in agony. Dying was better than this. Somehow or the other, she would kill herself. But why, she wondered now, had she said that to the khansamah? She shouldn't have.

After a while, Najma's moaning ceased.

The ship stopped. She looked through the porthole. The place looked familiar. She looked towards the ghat. Yes, certainly it was familiar. It was the ghat near Kalihati. The sand at the ghat was submerged. It was not yet noon. Two youths were sitting on the bank and fishing. Nearby was the path which led to Poramati. The fields and the surroundings seemed to recognize her. They beckoned to her to come to them. But could the villages have remained as they were? No. She gazed at the two fishermen. They seemed to be more interested in the ship than in their fishing.

After a while, Mehr saw the beast, along with two others, alight from the ship. He made his way to the fishermen and appeared to question them. Perhaps he was asking them for directions. She could not hear them as they were at quite a distance from her. However, she could guess from their gestures that they were asking for directions. After speaking to them, Kamaluzzaman and the others went off towards Poramati.

The two men on the shore continued fishing with their rods. There were two long ditches next to them. The beast and his demon companions must have gone to Poramati to continue their work of destruction in that area. She grew angry. If she could, she would have destroyed them immediately. But right now, she did not even have the right to die. The door was open. A sentry was guarding it. She could not commit suicide inside, nor could she go out and jump into the river. A guard was standing there. There was nothing she could do.

There was just that one thing that she could think about. Death. Any hope of preserving her chastity was now shattered. Any thought of marriage only brought anguish now. However, a single idea dragged her back repeatedly from death to the battlefield of life. It was the thought of revenge. If only she could somehow avenge herself on that monster, in some way! Only then could her soul find peace. Not just her own soul—the souls of many of Bangladesh's women would find peace.

But how could she avenge these wrongs done to her and to so many others?

Lying down on the bunk, she kept thinking of all this. At some point, she fell asleep.

She did not know how long she slept. When she awoke, she realized that the ship was sailing again. The weather was quite clear. She got up hastily and went to the porthole. She glanced out at her birthplace. The memories of her village seemed to be a dream. Babajan and Xoruma were gone. The village was as desolate as a graveyard. The tailor Kamal was gone to who knew where? The pond in their backyard was by now probably neglected, its banks overgrown with weeds. Nobody would be returning to that house again. This was probably her last glimpse of her birthplace.

Tears flowed from her eyes unconsciously. She gazed unswervingly at the land of her birth for a long time.

We herd the cattle in your fields,
We go to the ferry at the river bank,
The whole day, in your rural paths,
Alive with birdsong, shadowed,
In your paddy-filled courtyards,
Are spent the days of my life
Hai, hai, I die
O Mother, all my brothers
Are your herdsmen, your farmers.

The lines of the song came to her mind on its own. Ah, what peace. She had sung this song many times in the meetings of the Awami League. Along with other girls, she had sung this song in chorus many times at the public meetings in Tangail organized by Sheikh

Mujibur and Maulana Bhasani. But she had never previously realized that there was some magic in the emotion conveyed by this song.

O Ma, tor choronetey dilem moi matha petey
Dey go tor payer dhula
O Mother, I lay my head at your feet
Give me the dust of your feet,
That will be the jewel on my head.
O Mother, I shall lay this poor person's wealth,
All of it, at your feet,
Hai, Hai, I die,
I shall not buy ornaments any more
The wares of others,
It's only a noose
Around my neck.

Her birthplace vanished from her vision. Kalihati was far away. But the picture of another land, of another place of birth, came to her mind. It was the birthplace described in the song.

The noonday sun grew strong. The rainy season was about to end. At times, she could see cultivators in the fields. The paddy was about to ripen. There was no sign of people in the villages. Either there was no one left or they had all gone out to work. There was not a single woman to be seen. Vultures were flying in the skies above one village. There was a huge sound of crashing waves. The earth was speaking, the land was weeping.

Hai, hai, I die.

Softly, she began to sing the song. Gradually, the woman who had been asleep within her awoke through the melody of the song. For a while, she forgot her own sorrows.

After some time, a huge sandbar, not yet submerged by the waters of the river, came into view. Immediately, memories came to life. This was Bhuyanpur. Every year, in the winter month of Magh, in mid-January, when pilgrims would come for a holy dip, there would be a huge mela here. The Hindus did not stay at home on that day. She, with her family would come to the fair too. All kinds of things were sold at the huge market in the fairground. The syrupy sweetmeat chomchom from Poramati, dolls depicting brides and grooms, ferris wheels, jatras, songs, dances and so much more! Her heart wept.

'Bibi Sahiba!'

Turning around, she saw the khansamah. In his hands was her lunch, along with a plate of sweetmeats. 'I've brought you chomchom from Poramati. Have it!' He arranged the rice and curry and the sweetmeats on the table.

Mehr did not even glance at them.

The khansamah said, 'Saheb told me to give you these sweetmeats from Poramati. I've brought them.'

'Take them away. I don't want them.'

With a sorrowful mind, she went to her bunk and lay down tiredly.

'Eat it. Saheb will get angry if you don't.'

Offended, Mehr said, 'Go and tell your Saheb that if he gives me poison, I will eat it. But I shan't eat the chomchom.'

The khansamah did not say anything. After a while, he said, 'Najma Bibi has stopped crying. When I told her about you, she asked many questions.'

'Hm.'

Mehr remained silent.

Not getting a response, the khansamah left. Mehr lay on the bunk, motionless and silent. But sleep eluded her. The food remained on the table. A fire burnt fiercely within her, consuming her being. She had lost faith in herself, even her faith in Allah. She was caught in a place between life and death. There was no light in this place.

Neither was there darkness. It was Kaalsondhya, an inauspicious twilight. Only death could save her now. How could she die? How could she take her own life? Through the open door, she looked out at the shimmering blue waters of the Jamuna.

Suddenly, she felt an urging in her mind. 'Run. Run away!'

In those waters there was peace. Eternal peace.

The water was at least ten feet away. It was a huge ship. The sentry would fire. Good. Let him. Why had this easy plan not come to her mind yesterday? She would not have been humiliated, shamed, if she had thought of it then.

She got up, and gathering together all her mental strength, prepared to run.

Suddenly, there was the sound of firing. The entire ship shook. She closed her eyes. They must surely have seen her. She prepared to die.

After a while, her awareness returned. The firing continued but she was unharmed. Suddenly, the sentry at the door ran away screaming. There was pandemonium inside the ship. Bullets pierced through the cabin walls and fell near her bunk. There were shrieks and shouts all around. It was only then that she realized that the bullets were coming from somewhere else from outside the ship. An idea came to her mind. She closed the door and lay down. But her ears remained alert.

Suddenly, the khansamah entered. 'Bibi Sahiba!'

Mehr saw that the man was trembling with fear.

'What's happening?' She looked at him. His face was pale.

'The guerrillas have attacked and broken the cannon. It doesn't work at all. The captain was asleep. He has now ordered the soldiers to fire with machine guns.'

'Lie down,' she told him. He had closed the door in the meantime. He lay down on the floor.

'How many soldiers are here?' she asked.

'A quarter of a platoon. But what's the use of that? They were all sound asleep. The cannon has been shattered. They fired before the soldiers on the ship could take aim. I was sitting in the kitchen and watching. But I saw many soldiers fall to the bullets and came away. There are no soldiers this side, so there's less to fear here.' Gradually, he stopped babbling.

She could not make out how much time passed. Perhaps it was about an hour. The sound of bullets still continued. Mehr suddenly stood up, though the khansamah was still trembling with fear. Gathering up her courage, she went out of the cabin. Once outside, she noticed that the fiend had taken up his position at the machine gun on the other side and was firing it.

With him were four other soldiers. They were firing automatic rifles. She looked on the other side of the cabin. She saw that two overseers were huddled together not too far away. They were staring at her. The sandbank was not visible from where she was. As soon as she saw their faces, Mehr knew that these workers were Bengalis. In their lungis and singlets, they were huddled together like wolves in the undergrowth . She went to Najma's door and knocked softly. At first, there was no sound from inside. But after a while, somebody shouted in great terror, 'Who is it?'

'It's me, Mehr,' she said, very slowly, distinctly and softly.

The door opened. Mehr saw Najma's pale face and her dishevelled hair. Neither of them could speak. Mehr noticed that Najma's face resembled withered leaves, completely bereft of green, of life. It was like a wilted rose, it was like the dimness of dusk. There was no ray of light on it.

Najma stood immobile for a while. She could make out nothing of what was happening. She was unable to distinguish whether this was a dream or reality. Why were these guns being fired? Why had Mehr come to her? Why was she forced to stay alive? None of this made any sense to her. Mehr, too, was in a similar condition. She understood what was happening, but could not comprehend how she had remained alive all this time. Her mind was swaying between life and death.

Najma could not believe her eyes. But when she finally realized that it really was Mehr in the flesh standing before her, all her pent up anger, rage, shame, humiliation and grief welled up in her. Blood rushed to her head. With a sudden and unnatural scream she fell down on the floor.

Mehr was stunned. She knelt down and placed her mouth near Najma's ears. Addressing her as her older brother's wife, she gently said to her, 'Najma Bou, it's me, Mehr.'

There was no answer. Mehr stood up and looked around the cabin for some water but found none. Agitated, she went outside. Without caring for the dangers around her, she went straight up to the two Bengalis and said, 'Give me some water. Otherwise Najma Bou will die.'

The two men looked at each other. Then one of them got up. In a spouted container to one side of the ship was a little water. This he brought to Mehr. She came back to the cabin.

The khansamah, who had been lying down, got up and came to Najma's cabin as well. Mehr was sprinkling water on Najma's face. The water in the container finished but Najma did not regain her senses. Mehr did not know what to do. She looked helplessly at the khansamah. He was examining Najma closely. He then gently took her hand and felt her pulse. He, too, looked at Mehr, not knowing what to do next. She got up to bring some more water. But just then, the two Bengali men came and stood at the door of Najma's cabin.

Mehr said, 'We need more water.'

They had brought water. Mehr took the container from them and began to pour the water on Najma's head. The khansamah felt Najma's feet. There was no warmth in them. Leaving Mehr there, he went to where the two overseers stood. The two of them were looking out towards the raging battle. The khansamah did not say anything. He was trembling with fear again.

Mehr did not know what was happening, who was firing or who was winning. She could not make out the contours of the battle. But she was not too hopeful. Seeing Najma's condition, her head began to spin. Her body, remembering the torture inflicted on it by that fiend, quivered. She had not eaten anything since yesterday. The platter of rice and curry and the sweatmeats from Poramati lay as they had been placed even now. Her nostrils were filled with a vile, loathsome smell even then. It was the smell of liquor on the fiends's breath. She felt nauseous. Her head was spinning.

Slowly, she went to where the two Bengalis had been a while ago. With difficulty, she held on to the railings and stood. But her body was very weak. Her thoughts were confused and hazy. She felt as though the blood had stopped coursing through her veins. She felt very dizzy. As soon as she looked down at the water, it seemed as though everything was spinning. The ship, the nearby village of Bhuyanpur, the whole of creation–everything seemed to be whirling. Everything seemed hazy.

Suddenly, she heard someone say, 'They are finished.' Perhaps, he meant the soldiers.

But she had no strength left to rejoice. Her ability to grasp what was happening, too, was weakening. All she could think about now was Najma Bou. A light-hearted, beautiful, lively girl had gradually changed into a mass of tortured flesh, totally drained of any joy or life. Breathing had become difficult for her and she had lost consciousness. In fact, on seeing Mehr, instead of regaining her mental balance, she had been wounded even further. And yet, just a few days ago, she had shared a bed with this same girl, slept under the same mosquito net, talking and laughing. Perhaps Najma had wanted to die out of shame and humiliation. Now Najma had got exactly what she wanted. But she herself had not got anything that she wanted. How was she even alive? She did not know.

After a while, she could no longer hear the sound of firing. The two Bengalis had also left. The khansamah, too, had vanished. It seemed the battle was over. The fiend was screaming with pain at the other end of the ship. She heard the sound of many people coming on board. The ship that she was on was at the rear of the fleet. Those ahead were smaller. She heard the sound of marching feet on them as well. Many people clustered together on the bank of the river. She could see all this, but everything seemed unreal and distant to her, as though she was viewing it on the screen of a cinema hall. Her heart was still thudding loudly. She could not understand yet that somebody had come to give her life and freedom.

Suddenly, a gun-toting young man in trousers walked towards her. At his approach, Mehr's instinct was to flee. But where could she hide? The weak sunlight of late afternoon fell on the deck. She looked down and waited.

'Baideo.'

On hearing the voice, which had addressed her as 'elder sister', instead of feeling relief, Mehr's anguish increased. A stifled sob escaped her.

'Baideo. Come along. It's me, Sameer.'

Wiping away her tears, Mehr said, 'Go away. Leave me, all of you. Let me die right here. Like Najma Bou . . .'

Sameer had probably heard of Najma Bou's death by now. But possibly he had not known that Najma Bou had wished to die. She had not felt the need to continue living. Mehr, too, wished to die. She was desolate because she could not.

Sameer said sympathetically, 'How can you be defeated by just this bit of cruelty, Baideo? The Khan soldiers will feel even more encouraged. It is much better to die fighting. Come on now. There's no time to brood over your condition and your sorrows. We've captured a lot of arms and ammunition. We have to take them all to a safe place. Time is very short. Come, that's a good girl, just follow me.'

The fiend was screaming even then in painful supplication. The sound of that pain seemed to give Mehr some inner strength. The feeling of revenge that had filled her dissolved into an unknown affection as she looked towards Sameer's face. Her need to avenge was satisfied.

Sameer silently lit up a cigarette. Puffing on it, he looked closely at the pain-wracked body of the fiend.

Suddenly, the monster shrieked, 'Water, water, water!'

Throwing away his cigarette, Sameer asked Mehr, 'Is there water, Baideo?'

Pointing towards Najma's cabin, Mehr said, 'There should be water in the container there.'

Entering the cabin, Sameer was startled to see Najma's pale, lifeless body. As he stared at her, the thought suddenly came to him—why should those who were responsible for the shame and humiliation of people like Najma be nursed? Why should their pain be alleviated? Let them die in supplication, in terrible agony. Even though he had picked up the container of water, he kept it back again.

The fiend was still screaming, 'Water! Water!' By then, there were many people on the ship. They were collecting rifles, bullets, LMGs and other arms and ammunition. Nobody bothered to quench his thirst.

Mehr suddenly felt a wave of pity for him. She remembered her act of giving water to the dying Yakub. She asked, 'Sameer, why didn't you get the container of water?'

Sameer replied angrily, 'Let him die, the fiend. Let him suffer. Let him pay the price, every bit of it, and only then die.'

At first, Mehr agreed with what Sameer was saying. But at the very next moment, her mind could not bear this. She said, 'Sameer, go and pour some water in his mouth.'

Surprised, Sameer looked at Mehr. He asked, 'So you have forgiven him? Them?'

Without a moment's pause, Mehr replied, 'One should not hate even an enemy when he is dying. Give him a drop of water to drink before he dies. Khoda will assess him on the Day of Judgement.'

It seemed to Sameer that it wasn't Mehr who he was listening to, but to the words of Jesus Christ and Mahatma Gandhi. Where did she get the strength to forgive this tyrannical, villainous enemy?

He asked, 'You are able to forgive those who have tortured you so terribly?'

Mehr answered calmly, 'That's a very difficult question. I can't answer it. But it is good to give him water.'

Sameer did as she said and gave the fiend water. As soon as he drank it, his eyes began to close. For a long time, Sameer looked at the officer. Bullets had pierced his body in several places. But he had not been shot in his head or chest. It was perhaps because of this that he had taken some time to die.

A man had died. But he had died after committing wrongs. He had been changed by a cruel and inhuman machine into a fiend. He had surely shot dead many people of Bangladesh. He had dishonoured many girls and women. Yahya Khan had certainly transformed the soldiers of West Pakistan into devils.

Sameer returned.

Mehr had, in the meantime, recovered somewhat. It wasn't Sameer's understanding and obedience that gave her strength, but his sense of duty. There was no tortured sadness in his words and deeds anymore. His only satisfaction was in his work. In addition, she began to think that it was not so easy to die. Najma Bou had been totally tired of living. She had not wished to live at all. Sameer had in him the strength of the sanjeevani plant that revives and resuscitates. That strength had taken away Mehr's desire to die.

She had opened up some of her thoughts and feelings to him. He had consoled her as soon as she had expressed her wish to die. He had dismissed her wish casually. He had made circumstances easier to bear and made her want to live once more. She had asked him to give water to the dying fiend. He had carried out her wish out of affection for her. She felt that the usefulness of her life on this earth had not yet ended.

Sameer looked at her, and smiling, he said, 'We never thought that we would find you alive and unhurt. Tell me, how did you manage to survive?'

Mehr replied in a hurt voice, 'This body is no longer the same as it was before.'

Sameer looked at her. In these last few days, she had become very thin. Like a river in the dry season, she had become emaciated and wasted. But Mehr did not mean her physical body. She was talking about her body being polluted at the hands of the Khan soldiers.

In this country, since time immemorial, men had been telling women to protect their purity, the sanctity of their bodies. Religion too had these directives. Society had always advocated this. These were prescribed by men. Yet, it was women who had to fulfil their needs. Sameer knew all this. But men could not look at a woman who had been dishonoured with a gaze free of conventional modes. He did not know how these women could be brought back to live their normal lives again within the society they lived in. He did not know how they could be freed from the feelings of disgrace either, of having a blot on their characters which came to them at the same time and the ill feelings of men.

Sheikh Mujibur would be able to give them a new nation. But would he succeed in establishing a fine, new liberal society? He did not know.

Mehr tried to understand Sameer's thoughts but failed. She said, in quite a normal tone, 'Do you know why Ramchandra sacrificed Sita?'

Sameer replied, 'There's no Ram now, nor Ayodhya. Look, Baideo, they have harmed many of our sisters and mothers. That is why we are fighting them.'

Mehr replied in an agitated tone, 'Will you be able to return our honour to us? Will men agree to marry us now? No, you will not. You know why? Because once a woman's body is polluted that body can never become pure again.'

Sameer did not reply. After a few moments, he lit up a cigarette. From a corner of the ship, a stream of warm blood gushed from the body of a dead soldier and fell into the waters of the Jamuna. As he smoked, Mehr's questions created a tumult in his mind. After a while, he said, 'It's we who are responsible for this condition of women. That is, we men.'

Mehr looked at Sameer's eyes. She did not understand his words. She did not ask him any questions.

After a while, Sameer said, 'Let's go, Baideo. Staying here for too long is not without danger. We are going to Kalihati. We have to go to Madhuban from there.'

It was irrelevant to ask where they were supposed to go. Her eagerness grew when she heard that they were going to Kalihati. The hope of setting eyes on her birthplace overwhelmed her. He said again, 'Let's go.'

Mehr followed Sameer. As soon as they climbed down the steps of the deck to the lower floor, she saw how busy the guerrillas were. They were collecting the arms and ammunition and putting them on bullock carts on the river bank. A few small boats too were waiting near the huge Bhuyanpur sandbar. As soon as she stepped ashore, she saw many others of such small boats. Villagers from both sides of the river were at work.

Sameer went up from the sandy banks to the fields. He stopped beside a narrow path and said, 'Stay here for a bit. I'll bring you some tea and rutis.'

In a short while, he came back with tea and rutis as well as some boiled eggs. She had no idea where he had brought them from. Both of them sat down and ate the food. Gradually, dusk fell on the river bank. Along with it came a cool breeze. Mehr's body and mind gradually cooled. Sameer began to hum a song.

O Ma,
Goriber dhon ja aachhey tai dibo chorontolaye . . .
Oh Mother,
Whatever wealth this poor man has,
I shall offer at your feet.

Hai, Hai, I die.
I shall not buy in another's house,
A noose, in the name of jewels.
Hai, Hai, I die.

After a while, Sameer asked, 'What kind of man is the khansamah?'

'He's a good man,' said Mehr. 'Why do you ask?'

'He's been captured. There will be a trial. Habib was asking about him. The sarengs, the overseers have surrendered. They are with our people,' Sameer replied.

This was the first time that Habib had been mentioned. Mehr blushed. But she was also piqued that he had not come to her even though he was here. She asked, 'Is he here as well?'

'Yes,' replied Sameer, 'Habib said that he will not be able to come right now. He's asked you to go to him.'

'He must be having a lot of work, then?' Mehr said, vexed.

'He's the one in charge of this attack.'

Mehr was silent. But her vexation did not go away.

10

It was night by the time they reached Kalihati. They had to stay at the shattered mosque.

While coming they had seen some empty houses. Only the schoolhouse was lit with clay lamps. Not a single candle had been lit in the mosque. The light of two lamps lit up two broken minarets and an unbroken part of the concrete roof. A few people were sleeping inside. One or two of them were groaning. Sameer called out to one of them, 'Kamal!'

A very weak voice from one of those who were in pain asked, 'Who . . .?'

'It's me, Sameer. Are you feeling better?'

'No.'

Mehr asked, 'Who? Kamal?'

The tailor!

'What's wrong?'

Sameer said, 'Sit down. I'll tell you. They captured him on the very day that your house was destroyed. They took him right up to Tangail. They kept him under surveillance for the first two days. During that time, they questioned him repeatedly and tried to get some inside information about the guerrillas from him. They failed. After this, there was a trial. You can well imagine what happened at the trial. Death sentence. But the commander's advice was different. He said, 'He will of course have to be killed. But what do you think about killing him by taking out his blood? Many of our soldiers are in this area of Tangail. Many are injured. Some of them need blood. It will be good to put him to use in that way.'

'The instructions were carried out. There was so much blood taken from his body that he was practically dead. His eyes rolled up in his head. Taking him to be dead, it was ordered that he be buried. But by some turn of fate on that very night, we attacked Tangail. We brought away some arms and ammunition. We rescued Kamal from the hands of the man who was about to bury him and brought him here. He is still at death's door.'

Mehr's mind was weary. In her melancholy state, she could not bear to listen to him anymore or see the tortured people around her. Still, she controlled her feelings, and, taking the lamp, went up to Kamal as he lay on the floor and looked at his face. It was colourless and pale. Not just pale, there was no sign of any life in his face, his eyes and his cheeks. Even when he looked at her, there was terror in his eyes. Mehr sat down cross-legged near him.

In the meantime, more people entered the mosque. Sameer said to her, 'Mehr Baideo, stay near Kamal. I have some work to do. I'm going out.'

'What work?'

'I'm going to the school. There are some prisoners there. We have to make some arrangements about them.'

'Prisoners?' Mehr asked, surprised.

'Yes. We have fought and in Tangail we have defeated them. Many have also been taken as prisoners.'

Mehr could hardly believe her ears. She asked, 'But how have you been able to take them on?'

Sameer's eyes became excited. 'Why shouldn't we? We have to defeat them.'

Mehr gaped at Sameer, astonished. Where had Sameer got the self-confidence to think of defeating the powerful enemy? Even as she pondered on this, he melted into the darkness.

Kamal had been listening carefully to Mehr's questions. Now he looked at Mehr and said, very softly and slowly, 'Maybe you have forgotten how they killed your Babajan and Xoruma. I have heard what happened to you as well. As for me, I'm dead already. I am hanging on to life somehow. There is no treatment. I will surely die. Many have died. We have to fight. Don't have any doubts. Our fight is the path of Allah's.'

Abruptly, Kamal stopped. His eyes showed the pain he was in. Mehr was afraid. She said, 'Don't talk. Go to sleep.'

Kamal was quiet for a while. Mehr gently stroked his dry forehead with affection. Quite some time passed in silence in this way.

The entire Masjid resembled a burial ground. All this was undoubtedly the work of those soldiers. They had smashed the minarets.

Kamal spoke again. 'Even at the time of his death, your Babajan did not scream even once. When Xoruma was tortured and killed, she screamed. But Babajan took Allah's name and closed his eyes. I, too, wanted to die like him. I could not die then. I shall stay alive for just a little while more. My heart was seeking you. That's probably the reason you are here. You . . . you've thinned down a lot. I understand . . . they . . . you . . .'

His words stopped. Mehr could make no reply. She kept stroking his forehead.

Abruptly, the moon appeared in the sky. A patch of light fell on Mehr's face. She was ashamed. She was afraid to show this face even to the moon. When she remembered how that fiend had grasped her with brute strength, she felt defiled, polluted.

Kamal looked steadily at her face. He seemed to be able to guess all that had had happened. She felt ashamed once more. Slowly, he said, 'Don't ever forgive them.' With much effort, he lifted his hands and kept them in hers. He said, 'I had hoped to marry you.'

'I know,' said Mehr.

'Where will you go now?'

'I don't know.'

Kamal said, 'These people are our only hope now. They will not be able to bring back your Babajan, your elder brother, your Xoruma. But you will be able to return to this village on the strength of the might of these people. Don't forget me when you return. I shall not be able to forget you even in paradise. There will be a new tailor in the village. The broken huts will be repaired. You will till the land, plant crops, thresh paddy. You will go to fetch water from the pond. You will watch the jatra during the rains. Your husband will be at home, the babies will cry, you will celebrate Eid . . . I shan't be able to stitch clothes for the festival.'

A warm tear fell on Kamal's breast. He paused and then asked, 'Why are you crying?'

'I won't be able to return to this village again. I won't.'

'Why? Where will you find a village like this?'

'I can't. I can't bear it.'

Kamal became silent.

After a long time, he asked, 'So Habib will be taking you with him?'

'I don't know.'

'Haven't you met Habib?'

'I haven't met him since that day. He doesn't have the time, does he?'

There was pique in the tone of Mehr's voice. If Habib had come to meet her at Bhuyanpur for even a moment, she would have known that Habib loved her more than all the work he was engrossed in. His work was his priority. She did not say that he did not love her. He did love her, yes. But now, perhaps he loved Bangladesh more.

Kamal stared at her, astonished. After a pause, he asked, 'Why did he not come to you?'

Mehr did not reply.

Kamal said, 'He'll come . . . Why shouldn't he? Really, it's because of him that Siddiqui's bahini is so active in Tangail.'

Mehr's heart swelled with pride. She said, 'I know. But who shall I open my heart to? Xoruma is dead. I have no idea where Malobika is. Does he . . .'

She began to sob.

Kamal understood Mehr's feelings now. He said, 'I don't know. But don't be so sad. Do you remember the story of Zulekha, Mehr?'

'Yes. I remember.'

'She was married to a powerful man. But just see how she searched out Yusuf. Have faith in yourself. Just see what love can do. Who can quench the fire of the heart? Ahalya was a stone. She became human once again when the dust of Ram's feet touched her.'

Mehr did not reply. Talking had exhausted Kamal. Mehr told him now, 'Kamal, go to sleep. You will become weaker if you continue to talk.'

Kamal dozed off. Mehr got up and went to the courtyard of the mosque. The leaves of the mango trees trembled in the wind. The village gleamed in the moonlight. There was peace and quiet all around. Slowly, she went out to the path. The bronzed earth glistened with a golden glow. After a while, she turned left. Soon, she stood in her own backyard. It was all bare. Empty. It was just plain soil all around till the ends of the earth. The burnt timber lay on the foundation of the house. Fearfully, she went to the pond. There were fewer trees in the backyard. Somebody must have chopped down the trees and hauled them away, taking advantage of the lawlessness all around. At her approach, a jackal fled. The water in the pond was brimming over. She cleaned herself ritually and began to offer namaz.

She did not know how long she was there. Suddenly, she heard a voice, 'Mehr.'

Who was calling her? The voice sounded like Babajan's. She felt as though Babajan had come down from paradise.

'Babajan!' she called out, indistinctly.

But there was nobody around. She believed that Babajan had returned as a spirit to guard the homestead. She felt that he was calling out to her to come to him. The next moment, she saw a ray of moonlight dancing on the waters of the pond. It seemed as though Xoruma was a water spirit in there. She seemed to be calling Mehr, saying, 'Come, Mehr, come.'

Mehr went forward, a step at a time, to the edge of the pond. Immediately, she felt as though something was dancing in the pond. The sound of the cricket came floating from the forest as though it was a melody played on a two-stringed dotara.

After a while, a bird that had been sitting on the branch of a jackfruit tree flew off to the skies with a loud flapping of its wings. It was as though a helicopter that had taken off. Her heart broke with a burden of dreadful grief. A breeze raised ripples on the water of the pond. The moonbeams broke up into slivers and scattered all around.

Suddenly, somebody called out, 'Mehr.' The voice came from close to where she was standing.

She turned around, but saw nobody.

It was desolate there. She turned back. Walking very fast, she did not stop till she was right inside the mosque. She called out, 'Kamal!'

Kamal was awake. He asked, 'Where did you go? To visit your home?'

'Yes.'

Kamal said, 'But you said you had no attachment to this village anymore.'

'I don't know why, but I wanted to go. I seemed to hear Babajan's voice calling me. He kept saying, "Mehr, Mehr!" I saw Xoruma too. She had turned into a water spirit. I saw a Mosondori! That fish-shaped spirit seemed to be calling me. I was scared.'

Kamal listened to her in silence. He then said, 'Sit.'

Mehr sat down cross-legged as before.

'I know you can't die,' he said. 'You will have to remain alive. Now get some sleep. Sameer will not be returning tonight. We shall have to go to the jungles of Madhuban tomorrow in the morning itself. From there we will have to go to the Garo Hills. Habib and his companions have captured a huge amount of arms and ammunition. That will all have to be taken. Siddiqui has given orders for us to leave this place by noon. The Khans will be coming here for sure after that.'

'Where is Siddiqui Sahab?'

'In the school-house. Sameer is there as well.'

'Go to sleep. I'll sleep as well.'

'Aren't you hungry?'

'Yes, I am. But there's nothing available now. It's okay. I don't need anything.'

Mehr stretched out on the cement floor of the mosque, her head opposite Kamal's. In a few moments, she was fast asleep.

The bullock cart stopped. Kamal was carried out from it on a stretcher. He was no longer speaking. His body was becoming cold.

Mehr had accompanied Kamal. Somebody came and said to her, 'You will have to get down.'

'Where is Sameer?' asked Mehr. She was still not fully awake. The man was wearing a pair of soiled khaki trousers and shirt. A scarf was tied on his head and he had a rifle on his shoulders.

'Whom do you mean? Sameer Biswas?'

The man smiled. He had a fair, shining face. Mehr stared at him with surprise.

'He has gone to battle. Who knows when he will return?' said the man. 'You go on ahead. You will come to a camp just a little way from here.'

'Where are they taking Kamal?'

'To a hospital.'

'Hospital?' Once more, Mehr was surprised. These last two days, they had been travelling by boat and bullock cart. They had come across several villages on the way. Everywhere they had met Mukti

Bahini soldiers in lungis or trousers. The Khans had not yet been able to enter the villages in the Tangail and Mymensingh areas. Those who sympathized with the enemy were lying low.

Mehr looked around. The area was thickly forested. This spot could not be seen from beyond the trees. The man pointed out a little path to her. She went down this path and came to a cluster of tents. It was drizzling.

There was a line of people who had just arrived there. She noticed Kamal being taken inside one of the tents. Looking at the other people, she suddenly saw Lutfur and the khansamah among them. Seeing her, Lutfur nodded his head. He was downcast. The khansamah was trembling. A few other prisoners were standing there. The lungi-clad man directed her to move forward. Her card would be seen in the next camp.

When she reached the camp, she saw a corpse lying there. It was all swollen up. She looked very carefully at the body and finally realized who it was. There was nobody else in the camp at that time. She came away from Najma's dead body. A foul odour was emanating from it. Why had the corpse been brought here?

When she walked on a bit more, the reason became clear to her. A doctor and an old man were coming. When they came near, the old man on seeing her said with astonishment, 'You are still alive?'

Mehr looked down. It was Najma Bou's elderly husband. He looked at the corpse from a distance. The doctor began to examine the body.

'You are here?' asked Mehr.

The man pointed to his right shoulder and leg and said, 'That day, after leaving the village, we attacked a ship. I was hit by a bullet. Ismail died. Nothing happened to anybody else. We won.' He sighed and then continued, 'I stayed for a long time in the hospital. I am all right now. But I was feeling really sad about what has happened back home and in the village. The old woman was killed. They took away Najma and you . . .' The old man's words choked up.

Mehr wanted to tell him how Najma Bou had died. But she stopped herself. She felt a deep self-loathing when she even remembered that scene.

The old man addressed her affectionately, 'Ai, I understand. There's no need to speak about these things. Allah will see to it that they suffer even more than this.'

Tears came to Mehr's eyes. She said, addressing him respectfully as elder brother, 'What is this place, Dadajan?'

'Madhuban. It was full of tigers and other wild animals. Previously, it was a den of dacoits. It is now a guerrilla camp and has a hospital.' The old man looked at Mehr and out of the blue asked, 'Did you meet Najma?'

Mehr looked down and replied, 'We were in the same boat. But we only met just before she died.'

'Roushana?'

'They threw her into the river. The fiend who did that fell to the guerrillas' bullets later. And Najma Bou! I heard her screams one day and realized that she was in a cabin near mine. I sent a message through the khansamah, telling her to be patient. I had expected to die myself. But fate had something else in store. She died, I survived. When she saw me, Najma Bou just collapsed. I poured a lot of water on her face and head. I tried to revive her. But she did not live.' Mehr's voice was choked. 'Where did Elder Bou die?' she asked.

'In the field,' said the old man. Silently, he looked up, skywards. Without a word, he went towards Najma's body. Mehr followed.

The young doctor had finished his examination and had covered the body with a cloth. He glanced at them as they approached, but did not say anything. Entering the camp, he washed his hands in a basin. After he had finished, he said to the old man, addressing him as 'uncle', 'Chachajan! I have seen torture, but never anything of this kind. I am ashamed to say it. The child in her belly is dead. She was badly bruised all over her lower belly.'

Nobody said anything. The doctor then looked at Mehr, and asked, 'Do you have a card?'

Without speaking, Mehr took out the card that Habib had given her from inside her blouse.

The doctor read the card in silence. Then he said, 'You will have to stay here.'

Mehr said nothing.

The old man asked, 'Does she need medical attention?'

'I'll have to examine her. It's time to bury the dead body now.'

The doctor called out. Immediately, two boys wearing lungis appeared. The doctor told them to take away Najma's body for burial and told the old man to go with them. Mechanically, the boys took away the corpse.

Back in the village, when the dead were taken to the graveyard, the last journey was always a sad one. It was always an event of great significance, with mourners weeping. There would be a tumultuous gathering of people who would come to condole and mourn. The immediate family would be too caught up in this to have time to even grieve properly. But the family would get some solace in the way people gathered around to be with them in the time of their grief. They would think that even though their family member was no more, at least the villagers were with them. The last rites would be performed for the dead person. This would be followed by a feast. Today, death was plain, without any of these ceremonies. The last rites would be conducted in a very basic manner. The whole country was now one terrifying graveyard.

The old man sat down for a while. He began to sob loudly.

Unable to bear the sight, Mehr looked helplessly at the doctor. He said, 'You go. I am writing it down . . . you will find people in the next tent.'

Mehr bade farewell to the old man. 'Dada, I am going.'

'Go, Ai,' he said, addressing her as his daughter. 'Go.'

Mehr left slowly and stood in front of the next tent. Hearing her footsteps, a young girl came out. When Mehr handed over her card to her, she examined it closely. 'Are you from Kalihati?' she asked.

'Yes.'

'There's another girl from Kalihati with us here. Her name is Malobika. Do you know her?'

Mehr forgot her grief. She had never imagined that she would meet Malobika in this hospital in the middle of the jungle. She said, 'Malobika was my neighbour. Is she all right?'

The girl replied, 'No, she is not all right.'

'Is she seriously ill?'

'No, she's not seriously ill either.'

'Then what . . .?'

'It's an illness of the mind.'

The girl examined Mehr's face closely. Mehr too looked at her. She saw that the girl was very beautiful. A young woman of this kind could only be seen in the aristocratic families of Dhaka. Her face was lovely. Her teeth were dazzlingly white. She looked very attractive in her dotted grey sari and red blouse. She was probably the same age as her. Mehr felt an affinity with her immediately. The other girl probably felt something similar. In an affectionate voice, she said, 'Come, come on in.'

The girl addressed her with the familiar 'Tumi', the word for 'you' which denoted affection and closeness. Mehr was overwhelmed. As though under a spell, she entered the tented shelter. There were several camp cots inside. There were probably more girls there. She felt better. She said, 'Please keep addressing me as Tumi.'

'How can it be that only I keep addressing you as Tumi? You must address me as Tumi as well. Isn't it?'

Mehr blushed with embarrassment. She said, 'All right, I will.'

'Sit down. You've come a long way. Aren't you hungry?'

Mehr nodded. The girl began to make tea. She put some water to heat on a stove. She said, 'There is some toothpaste on the table. Go and wash your face.'

Mehr saw that there was a little mirror on a small wooden table. There was a comb, toothpaste and powder on it. The girl took the tube of toothpaste and put it in Mehr's hands.

Mehr asked, 'Why are you taking so much trouble just for me? I could have taken it myself.'

'Wah!' exclaimed the girl. 'Why would you do that, tell me?' There was a sweetly teasing tone in the girl's voice. She looked at Mehr with a charming sideways glance. In a moment, Mehr was totally beguiled. She asked, 'Why pamper an ordinary, unfortunate girl like me?'

'Wah, wah! What logic! So we are extraordinary? And people like me are fortunate, is it?'

The girl began to smile mischievously. She then said, 'Saying "no" is not permitted here. You have to say "yes". And nobody can be sad here. Everybody has to remain happy while they are here. The rules are very strict.'

In spite of the terrible sadness within her, Mehr had to laugh. She began to clean her teeth with the toothpaste. The girl gave her some water in a spouted container. Mehr went outside and washed her face and rinsed her mouth. In a little while, the girl brought some biscuits along with the tea and placed it in front of Mehr. 'Sit down on the bed and drink this.'

Mehr sat on the bed.With the cup in her hand, she asked, 'How can I have it all alone?'

'I've had mine quite some time ago.'

'No, unless you have some too, I shan't either,' said Mehr, determinedly.

'You really mean it?'

'Yes.'

'All right then. In that case, I'll have some.'

Mehr said, 'Where are the biscuits? You haven't taken any?'

'Wah! Oh, great! You've changed from a guest to a hostess already! In a few days, there won't be any place for us in this house! All right, I'll have some.'

The girl took some biscuits from a packet on a nearby shelf and came to Mehr.

Mehr's mind cleared up. After witnessing all those scenes of death, and after all the tortures she had borne, joy had vanished from her mind. She had thought this state of mind was now permanent. Now, suddenly, like the diurnal tide, joy had returned to her. She asked, 'What's your name?'

'My name is Syeda Amina Kamal. How do you like the name?'

Sipping on her tea, Mehr said, 'It's great. You are a Syed?'

Amina replied, 'Forget all that. We are now daughters of Bangladesh. There are no such things as Syed-Hanifa, Shia, Sunni, Hindu-Muslim, Brahmin-non-Brahmin, rich-poor. We are now all just 'children of Golden Bangla. Shonar Bangla.'

Mehr said seriously, 'It's not yet time for us to be able say that.'

The smile dried up on Amina's face. She finished her tea and hastily placed the cup on the floor. She then asked, 'We cannot say Ma, Mother?'

'No.'

'Why?'

Mehr, too, placed her cup on the floor. She said, 'I cannot imagine that. My mind is full of dead bodies. I, too . . .' She could not finish her sentence.

Mehr's voice trembled. She was meeting another woman after a long time. And yet she could not talk openly of the grief in her heart. Malobika, the daughter of the Brahmin of Kalihati, was screaming. Every now and again, Najma Bou was screaming from the boat's cabin. Xoruma was crying out loudly from the pond in her house. She herself was inside a cabin. Every now and again, she sobbed in agony after the purity of her body was stripped from her. Would she ever be able to get back her body again, unpolluted and unsullied? She could not speak openly about this grief to anybody else. Not even to another girl.

Amina smiled a little. Perhaps she got an inkling of the sadness in Mehr's mind. She said, 'Will our country be liberated if we just sit around feeling sad? You and I, we have to sacrifice everything we have. Only then can there be fulfilment at the end of it all. What you have already given—even that will not be enough. You will have to give your mind and soul—everything else as well.'

Stunned and astonished, Mehr stared at Amina. She was urging an ordinary girl to extraordinary deeds.

Just then Dr Momin came and stood at the door of the camp. He was young and sweet-faced. He had studied abroad. He said, 'Amina, in just ten minutes it seems both of you have become great friends. Girls are very good at this!'

Amina answered easily, 'If only politics was also left in our hands, we would have brought Bangladesh into existence just by talking with each other. Instead of Yahya Khan, if Miss Fatima Jinnah had been the president, this terrible war would never have happened. What do you say?'

A smile lit up Amina's face like a flash of lightning. Momin was a shy man. He never spoke much. However, he was caught in Amina's playful reply. Smiling, he said, 'There's no time left to talk now, is there? After Bangladesh comes into being, try to become the president.'

Amina began to laugh. She knew the doctor's temperament. He was never inclined to talk much about anything other than work. Nor did he have the disposition. After a few moments, the smile on his face was replaced by a serious look. He said, 'I notice that some very beautiful roses are blooming in your garden. Najma Bou, the woman who was brought in a while ago, has been given a burial. The old man is weeping so much. I haven't heard of this kind of torture anywhere, at anytime in history. I had heard a lot of stories about the Nazis when I was in Europe. But even they had not committed this kind of savagery, this kind of brutality. There are terrible wounds in her belly, her breasts . . . Go and put some flowers on her grave.'

Amina replied, 'I'll go and do that right away.'

'Yes.' He indicated Mehr and continued, 'After that, bring her to the examination room. I am going there.'

'Malobika is her friend!' said Amina.

'Is that so? You must be from Kalihati then?'

'Yes,' responded Mehr.

The doctor said worriedly, 'She's lost her sanity. Sometimes she laughs without any reason. At other times she screams without any cause. There are no arrangements here for psychiatric treatment. We are trying to send her to India. We can't do anything here.'

Saying this, the doctor went away. His head was bent down. Mehr and Amina looked at each other. There was no smile on either of their faces. A cloud of sadness had descended on them.

11

Mehr saw here that along with graves, war and torture there also existed flowers, music and poetry. On the very first day, Dr Momin examined her and gave her medicines. Even though she had lost her virginity, she had got back the life of a girl again. But the burden of shame, of being stigmatized, had not gone from her mind yet.

Nobody spoke of stigma, of shame here. The girls looked after the sick. The doctors treated them. During their free time, the doctors, nurses and patients would sit in the garden and talk their hearts out. This was a totally different world. A beautiful world was being created in Madhuban. This was not like the rural homesteads of Kalihati. It was not like the quarrels between two dissimilar wives in the home of the old man of Islampur either. There was no fear here of the beastial torture that had occurred on the boat. The place was surrounded by soldiers of the Mukti Bahini. The Khan soldiers had not been able to penetrate this place. It was a two days' journey to Assam from here.

A clear moonlit night. The nurses had decorated the shelter with flowers. They had decided to have an evening of songs. Amina had told her that there would be recitations of poetry as well.

Suddenly, Najma's husband came looking for Mehr. The old man had recovered completely. In his hands was a bundle containing odds and ends.

'Mehr.'

Mehr came out from the shelter, and asked, 'Dadajan, are you leaving?'

'Yes.'

'Where will you go?'

'To fight. There's no point staying here any more. Bangladesh will have to be liberated.'

Mehr sighed. She asked, 'Dadajan, will you really be able to defeat them?'

The old man looked at Mehr for a long time. Addressing her with the familiar 'Tui', finally he said, 'I have heard everything about you. That is why I am addressing you as "Tui". You are the daughter of Amir Ali Saheb. I knew him very well. We worked for the Awami League. We moved around together during the elections. I had met your elder brother Muhiuddin as well. Your father was a great man. Being his daughter, how can you ask such a question? I see that you still have some doubts! You are not aware of what's happening in this war. The Khan soldiers have not yet been able to enter Mymensingh, Tangail and Rongpur. They have now gathered together in the big cities. Our young men are fighting day and night. There's no reason for us not to win. If I just sit around, I will be sinning. I have nobody. I only have my country now.'

Mehr said, 'Come, I will see you off.'

'Come along, then.'

After walking for a while, the two of them stood beside Najma's grave. Mehr was wearing Amina's dotted sari. A rose gleamed in her hair. Her face looked beautiful with its light makeup. Conch shell bangles jingled on her wrist. Smiling, the old man asked, 'Have you been able to rid yourself of your mind's illness, Mehr?'

Mehr paused for a moment, then replied, hesitatingly, 'I am all right now, Dadajan. But . . .'

'Tell me. You can tell me without fear.'

Mehr blushed. She wished to send a message to Habib. But she could not bring herself to say it out. Instead, she said, 'No, it's all right.'

The old man began to laugh. He said, 'Just think of me as your mother-father-grandfather–everybody.'

'How can you be so many people? I have nobody.'

The old man said, 'I don't have anybody either. And yet, I do. Has the water of the Jamuna ever dried up? The water keeps flowing. That's the law of the world. For those who have left this world, a drop of water from the eyes. That's it. Try to lighten your mind, like Amina.' He paused. 'Kamal's bed was next to mine. He is not well at all. He could speak only about you. He loves you a lot. Oh yes, he told me everything about you. What can you hide from me, you foolish girl?' he said affectionately.

Surprised, Mehr asked, 'You can be so concerned about me?'

'Yes. I am human too. One can love Allah and one's country if one can love one's fellow humans. Why should I not be concerned about you? In this place, everybody is concerned about everybody else. Why are you embarrassed before me?'

For the first time Mehr felt that this was not the time to keep herself and her mind in check. The mind, after all, was not a pond. It was more like a river. The pond had burst its banks. It was as though the Brahmaputra had flown out from the cave after Parasuram's axe had cleaved the mountains.

Mehr asked, 'Will you be meeting Habib?'

'Yes, I will. I shall be going to him. He's the son of Badaruddin of Tangail after all. His father and I had a jute business together. I've heard that you are very much in love with him.'

Mehr blushed. 'Who told you?'

'Kamal. Do you want me to carry a message for him?'

Mehr was glad. There was nothing to hold her back here. Rules and regulations that had tied people back home were not applicable here. In this hospital, people lived a free life. Nobody thought of her here as a woman with a stain on her character. Everybody had an affectionate look on their faces. Smiling, she said, 'Tell Habib that I am here.'

'That's all? Nothing else?'

Gathering together all her courage, Mehr said, 'Dadajan! I have a question.'

'What is it? Tell me,' the old man asked affectionately. His beard shone. His eyes had a calm and tranquil look. His face, like that of fakirs, was suffused with a glow that spoke of detachment from the world. He seemed to be like her father, someone who would understand her emotions. Mehr had faith in him. She asked, 'Will Habib be disgusted with me, my condition?'

The old man's face became grave. He said, 'It's difficult to understand a man's mind. I can't say about Habib.'

Mehr asked, 'Dadajan, are all men like this? I get very angry about this at times. But I don't know who I'm angry with.'

Smiling, the old man said gently, 'I see that you're trying to change the minds of men also. It's only Allah who will be able to vanquish the lustfulness of men. Allah will be able to restore the honour of women. Have faith in Allah. I don't know of any other remedy besides this.'

Mehr realized that her new Dadajan was a man too. She felt saddened. Everybody's ultimate hope lay with Allah. But why was Allah witnessing this torture on women silently? Why?

She replied, 'I have faith in Allah. But will Allah do the work that was supposed to be carried out by men? Amina has studied in college. She's studied these issues. Do you know what she said?'

'What?'

'Men will never, on their own accord, give women equal rights.'

The old man began to laugh. 'I don't know about all that Mehr. Talk about it with Habib. He is educated. He is a person whose heart is with the people. Otherwise, why would he leave his job and join the Mukti Bahini? I'm leaving. I have to go a long way.'

Hurriedly, Mehr said, 'Don't mention any of this to Habib.'

'Why?'

'No, don't.'

The old man was surprised at Mehr's words. He said, 'Even the gods can't make out what's going on in a woman's mind. All right. I'll say–Mehr is calling you. Will that do? I'll only say that.'

Mehr wished to say something else, but the old man patted her on the back and took his leave in an easy manner. As he was going, he said, 'Don't be sad.'

Mehr stared at the old man as he walked away quickly. Gradually, he was lost to view in the forest. There was a sense of isolation near Najma's grave at that time. There were some more graves near her's. A patch of deep forest lay beyond the graves. Through this patch went a narrow, twisting path. Amina had told her that the guerrilla headquarters and prison lay in that direction. Only Amina, of all the nurses, had permission to go there. Sometimes, meetings would be held there. At times, people from the Awami League would come there. The liberation battles of this area were planned and directed from there.

The nurses were singing the song 'Shonar Bangla'. She had heard this song before. But today, the melody was very soft. Her mind, too, was especially receptive. She was sensitized to the song. The lyrics painted a picture in her mind. The blue skies above, the gentle breezes–it was as though everything was rousing new hopes in her soul. The scenes on the banks of the Jamuna came to her mind. The mango orchard, the play of light and shade in the depths of the jungles, the endless call of birds, both known and unknown, and in the midst of all this, a cheerless face! The visage resembled that of Xoruma. She remembered her home, glimmering in the lamplight of evening. Many children played around and within the homestead in the daytime. She could hear the shouts of the children as they returned home in the evening. Her mind then raced towards the river, the wharf for the ferries and boats, the village roads, the fields of golden paddy. She had always loved them. Perhaps it was because she was separated from them now . . .

She remembered a band of guerrilla fighters. They–

Suddenly, the sound of the song was drowned out by the sound of bullets. She realized that the sound was coming from the direction of the forest. Not just a single volley. There was the sound of many rifles being fired, volley after volley. After a while, it became quiet again The nurses' song, too, had stopped. Possibly the guerrillas were practising their shooting.

❀

Mehr observed that when Malobika saw her, she would talk normally for a while, but the very next moment, she would scream unnaturally. Whenever memories of being raped before her father's eyes, having her house burnt down, seeing her father die in front of her came to her, terror probably made her lose her mental balance. At these times, she looked completely mad. This unheard-of condition, this terrible state of the daughter of a father who meticulously observed all the religious rituals, was the same as being dead. For the daughter of a man who worshipped the holy Shaligram, the sacred ammonite that stood for Vishnu himself, this was the same as dying. When she was in the throes of a fit, she would try to kill herself by smashing her head against a heavy object. There was a guard near her at night. The doctor and nurses did not know what to do.

It was about ten at night. Mehr was sitting next to Malobika's bed looking after her. It was a moonlit night outside. The sleepless birds were calling out. The doctor had given her morphine and put her to sleep.

Suddenly, Malobika woke up with a strangled cry of pain. She opened her eyes. She saw Mehr, and said, 'Mehr, I am being called.'

'Who's calling you?' asked Mehr. 'I don't hear anything. You must have had a dream! Go back to sleep.'

Malobika sat up. In a harsh voice, she said to Mehr, 'Let me go. I am being called. You are punishing me.'

Mehr was very saddened. She went and sat close to Malobika. 'Aren't you happy that I am with you?'she asked.

Malobika stared back at her with a frozen, mute gaze. It was a totally blank stare. Her face shone in the lamp light. It was a calm, soft, sweet face, like a tuberose. Outside, thick with sadness, the silent night wept. A bird called out, 'Bou kotha kou.'

Gently, she stroked Malobika's hair, arms, face and back. Malobika stared at her for a long time and calmed down. She asked, 'What time is it, Mehr?'

Mehr said, 'It must be past nine, I think. Would you like something to eat?'

'No. I'm fasting. You don't know about it. It's the konyapukur fast. Has Baba returned? You know, Baba is going through a lot of trouble. He had gone to Pabna to look for a good groom for me.'

Mehr did not know what to say in reply. Even if this was the talk of a woman who had lost her mental balance, hearing it caused confusion in others too. Hesitatingly, Mehr replied, 'Your groom will surely come, Malobika.'

'Baba is so sad! Do you know what he said to me?'

'What?'

'Put your ear near my mouth, I will tell you.'

Mehr did as she was told. Malobika whispered, 'Baba says that god has fled from there. Come away from there, quickly, and bring the Shaligram with you. Mehr, will you take me to our house?'

'Yes, yes, I will. Now go to sleep,' said Mehr.

Tears fell from Mehr's eyes. She remembered the sounds of the kettle drum and conch shell every morning and evening. There would be many pujas throughout the year. Charak Puja in the month of March, the Poush Sankranti at the end of the month of Puh, in mid-January, Durga Puja in autumn, Lakshmi Puja every Thursday and indeed, so much more! As the saying went, there were thirteen festivals in twelve months. She had heard that when the zamindar Choudhury was in the village, the festivals had been celebrated with great pomp and splendour. After the creation of Pakistan, many Hindus, including the zamindar, were tortured and persecuted. Many died. Many fled to India. Their lands were taken over by the 'Bhag Chashi', those who gave them out to tenant farmers for a share of the crops.

Malobika's family did not go away. Guarding their precious Shaligram, they remained there with their Muslim brethren. Malobika's father was a teacher in the primary school. In his free time, he practised astrology. They got along well with everybody. Sometimes, her father would come to the front room of Mehr's home. On his forehead would glisten the lines of sandal paste. Sometimes, he would lament the bad condition of Hindus there. Lakhs of people had fled the country in fear of being persecuted. When the Awami League had come into being, a new wave of amity had swept their village. The Hindus could at last look people in the eye when they spoke.

Mehr would drop in to see Malobika frequently. When Malobika's father had to go to some distant river to take a holy dip there, or when he had to visit relatives, he left the house in the care of Mehr's family. On Eid, Mehr's father would send across apples, almonds and kishmish to the Brahmin's house. During Durga Puja, batashas, bananas and sweetmeats would come from Malobika's home to theirs. Religious strictures forbade the two families of different faiths from eating in each others' homes. Even so, though the people of the two houses did not dine with each other, there was no lack of goodwill among them.

Malobika said, 'Baba says that they will never be able to destroy the sacred Jogot Taran Narayan Shaligram that symbolizes the protector of the world. He has advised me to tie the sacred stone around my neck, and go away. Will you come with me?'

Mehr said, 'Let us wait till morning.'

Malobika looked suspiciously at Mehr and said, 'You also consider me to be mad. Just like the others. Sih, what deceit! I'll show you just now that I am not mad. You people are. You are the mad ones!'

Saying this, she got down from the bed. In a totally unexpected manner, she rushed to the door. The door was slightly ajar. She pushed it open and ran very swiftly into the courtyard.

Flustered, and not knowing what to do, Mehr shouted out as loud as she could. She rushed after Malobika. The quietude of the hospital was shattered. Nurses, doctors, patients—everyone came running out.

Malobika was running breathlessly from the courtyard towards the well. Mehr panicked. The other people looked on, stunned. But only for a few moments. They too followed Mehr. It would be appalling if she jumped into the well. Just before Malobika reached the well, Mehr grabbed her hand. But Malobika began to pull away, screaming, 'Mehr, let me go!'

It was a scream of despair and hopelessness. Mehr could not hold on to her. Both of them slipped and fell on the muddy ground. Malobika collapsed with a thump. Her head banged against the large washing stone. Mehr, too, fell down. Malobika screamed out shrilly and fainted. Mehr had never heard such a scream before. Her heart quaked with fear.

In the light of the torches, Mehr saw that Dr Momin and a guard had lifted Malobika up. Her head was bleeding profusely. Somebody lifted Mehr up too. She saw that it was Amina. She was still wearing her day clothes. She must have been looking after some patients. She herself was covered in mud. Standing up, she started to walk back to the shelter. They reached their tent.

'Change your clothes,' said Amina.

After changing into clean clothes, Mehr lay down on her bed and began to think over all that had happened. She had been very frightened. Amina had not changed her clothes yet. She warmed a cup of milk and gave it to Mehr, then poured a cup for herself as well. When Mehr had calmed down, Amina smiled and said, 'Habib Sahab's patient. You did a very good thing by saving her. Habib had repeatedly told Dr Momin and me, "She will have to be saved. She will have to be made into a strong, healthy citizen of Bangladesh. We shall have to give back this Hindu girl her honour. We shall have to live as one race."'

Habib's name acted as a tonic for Mehr. She sat up and asked, 'Do you know Habib?'

'Who doesn't know him? Habib is just behind Bagha Siddiqui. He is the leader of the guerrillas of Mymensingh-Tangail.'

'Does he come here?'

'Yes, he does. Why?'

Mehr did not reply. She remained staring at Amina. Looking back at her silent gaze, Amina said again, 'This is where the guerrillas are trained. There will be an assembly here next Friday. He is sure to come. The rainy season is about to end. They are drawing up big plans to free Bangladesh.'

Mehr asked with great curiosity, 'How do you know all this?'

'I am a guerrilla as well. Besides, we shall have to fight this war all together, shoulder to shoulder.'

'Do you know how to fire a rifle?'

'Yes, I do. Rifles, hand grenades, LMGs.'

It was all like a story, a fiction for Mehr. Amina said, 'A large group of armymen are searching everywhere for us. At some point, we might be required to fight them. They have come to know that we have a camp here. Therefore . . .'

Amina conveyed the rest of what she meant through the expressions on her face. A determination crept into her eyes and face. She said, 'Mehr, listen! It is better to die fighting than to be dishonoured by the Khans.'

Instead of replying, Mehr now recounted her own experiences. She told her everything. How Habib had taught her to fire a revolver. How she had been defiled. The pain of being dishonoured that had been festering within her. She recounted everything. In the end, she said, 'I also wanted to die but could not. I feel that I am a prostitute now.'

Amina knew of this self-loathing from many other women in a similar situation. She was a well educated urban girl, free from the constraints of customary ways of thinking. She did not even deign to think that this was a problem. She asked, 'Mehr, why should you think yourself to be a prostitute?'

Mehr described Xoruma's, Najma's and Malobika's sufferings. Malobika had lost her mind because she had lost her purity. No matter what the reason, a woman who could not protect her honour considered herself to be lesser. Lower. Besides, men found it difficult to give a place to such women in their homes, or marry them.

Amina said, 'All this is just a confusion in your mind. Men will be encouraged to abandon you if you think of yourself as flawed, or low.'

Saying this, she got ready to go to the ward. Mehr wished to talk some more. But she could not. Amina said, 'Kamal is in a very bad state, he's almost at the end of the road. I'll stay near him through the night.'

Mehr was startled. She said, 'In that case, I'll come with you.'

'No. You go to sleep.'

Suddenly, they heard the roar of planes in the sky. Amina listened intently. Sometime later, they heard the sound of bombs being dropped not very far away.

Amina said, 'Go to sleep. It seems the attack has started.'

❀

That night, Malobika had a fit. Kamal died. And bombs destroyed quite a few of the houses in the guerrilla headquarters. In the prison camp, shrapnel from the bombs pierced the bodies of Lutfur and the khansamah of the boat. They were brought to the hospital in a critical state.

Kamal was buried near Najma's grave. Mehr did not eat anything that day. With Kamal's death, her relationship with her own village could be said to have ended. Even though Malobika was alive, she was not actually in this world. Dr Momin sent her to India the day after Kamal's death as her mental instability was not getting any better here. Mehr could not eat anything that day either. Even at the time of her departure, Malobika screamed, 'I am being called, Mehr! I am being called!'

Death was calling her. No. In a way, she was already dead. Not even a drop of what she understood to be life remained in her. Her Brahmin-ness, her virginity, her home, her father, her hopes of a marriage, a calm mind–she had lost them all. She could not live in any other way. And so, she too was dead.

In her grief, Mehr also felt that the relationship between herself and her village now lay scattered on the ground, like the fallen flowers from a garland whose string had snapped. All the faces, bodies, voices, glances that were dear to her were buried in the ground. Babajan had been burned to ashes. Xoruma had turned to sediment. She was one with the dregs in the pond. Najma Bou and Kamal had turned to dust in their graves. They were all becoming one with the earth. Malobika, too, would probably join them in a few days. She herself would also go one day. This earth, this land, was now her father, mother, her beloved, her friend.

The sky was calm that day. The weather clear. The earth was tranquil. Mehr had made tea and was waiting for Amina. Seeing that Amina had not come, Mehr decided to go the ward herself. She put the tea kettle on the stove and walked slowly towards the Surgical Ward. She stopped when she heard people conversing inside. Dr Momin and Amina were talking very softly to each other. There were no patients in the Surgical Ward that day.

Mehr wanted to return. Suddenly, Dr Momin's agitated voice came to her ears. 'I can't go on, Amina! If I carry out operations in this way, it will be the same as killing them. There are no instruments, no anaesthesia, no helpers. I can't do it.'

Amina said, 'You have to be able to do it. You will be able to do it. I know you.'

Dr Momin replied, 'Am I Dhanvantari, Amina? Am I that person who we believe had founded the Hindu system of medicine?'

Amina replied, 'You are much more than Dhanvantari. The operation you performed on Najma's husband was a very difficult one, wasn't it? A bullet in the shoulder. A bullet in the leg. I was very impressed when I saw you working that day. The battle you fought to save a freedom fighter of Bangladesh, to save a human life, is no less a battle than the one fought by Habib, Siddiqui and the others. That day itself I . . . your . . .'

'My?'

'Your . . . mine . . .'

Mehr could not catch what was said next. Suddenly, a tender agitation crept into Momin's voice. 'Amina, do you really love me?'

'Do I have to swear to it?'

'No, you don't.'

'Look. No other man has impressed me so much. They killed Babajan on the 25th of March in Dhaka. I fled the place that very day with a rifle in my hands. But no women's force was created. Habib told me to come to the hospital. I was unhappy here at first. What kind of war could be fought here? I was worried. But in these four and a half months, an actual battlefield has been established. You are the commander.'

Momin could not say anything. He was a shy person.

Mehr returned to the tent. In a little while, Amina, too, returned. 'Is the tea ready, Mehr?' she asked.

'The tea has overboiled. It's become bitter. I'll make it again. Since you were late, I went to call you and heard you talking. I'll make it. Sit down. What has happened to the doctor? Why doesn't he want to operate anymore?' There was a mischievous smile on Mehr's face.

Amina's face took on the hue of the setting sun. Pretending to be angry, she said, 'It's not proper to listen to others' conversation!'

'You think of me as an outsider, don't you?'

'No, I don't.'

'In that case?'

Amina lay down sideways on a bed, and said, 'I liked you from the very first day that we met. I have never felt that way with anybody else before.'

Mehr made the tea. Placing it along with some biscuits on a cane murha near Amina, she said, 'Have your tea first. There's nothing else today.'

Amina got up and began to sip her tea. Mehr asked, 'Will you address me as "tui"?' referring to the intimate mode of address.

'Certainly. You do the same, as well. There's a condition though. You can't tell anybody about all this.' There was a happy smile on Amina's face.

'Why should I tell anybody? But why did the doctor say that he would not operate?'

Amina gulped down her tea. Lying down again, she said, 'Come, sit down. I'll tell you.'

Mehr sat down on the bed and began to massage Amina's head. Lulled by the soothing sensation, Amina closed her eyes for a while. Then she said, 'Lutfur and the khansamah are our prisoners. We have strict orders to look after the prisoners well. Lutfur was brought to the operating table in the afternoon. After examining him, the doctor realized that he was in a critical condition. He is wounded in the stomach, knee, and on the upper portion of his right arm. The doctor decided to enter the stomach first, to take out the splinters of the bullet and stitch him up again. But he saw that there was no anaesthesia. In fact, there was no disinfectant for his surgical instruments either. He did not operate. The khansamah was brought in after that. He was in an even worse condition. One of his thighs are shattered. His leg will have to be amputated. Again the problem was the same. The doctor was deeply troubled. He is very upset with Habib and the others now! He sat down in the operation theatre, without saying anything, for a long time. Later, he called me and said, "Amina, I can't continue any more." You must have heard some of the rest . . .'

Laughing, Mehr said, 'That bit of over-hearing, is that enough? I want to hear from you just how you treated such a respected, well known doctor like him.'

Amina replied, 'Treatment? No, not at all. I have never seen Dr Momin this depressed. I have never seen him speak badly to anybody, under any circumstance. He has never thought of any kind of scarcity as a deterrent. He has never acknowledged hardship to be a problem. He has never been disheartened. But he could not stop himself today. At times like this, even the gods cannot. He did actually want to give up this work and leave today. That would have led to the closure of the only hospital for Bangladesh's fighters. I could not take it. I gave my all to that dejected god and brought back his strength.'

'How much did you have to give him, tell me?'

'Dhet! You're very naughty.'

Unexpectedly, Mehr recalled the warm, honeyed, indescribably delicious kiss that Habib had given her on the cheek when they were coming away from Kalihati. She grew absent-minded. She withdrew her hand from Amina's forehead.

'What's the matter with you? Tell me.'

'No, nothing is the matter.'

Amina examined Mehr's face carefully, and asked, 'Tell me, what's wrong? Are you remembering your heart's beloved?'

Somehow, in great embarrassment, Mehr managed to reply, 'Yes.'

'So who is he, this man?'

Shyly, Mehr whispered the name in Amina's ear. Amina began to laugh.

But their conversation had to end at that point. Dr Momin came and stood at the door of the camp, and said, 'Amina, come to the operation theatre. I have decided to use morphine in place of anaesthesia. Besides, I have thoroughly cleaned up and sterilized the surgical instruments. I will operate on Lutfur first.'

Obediently, Amina got up from the bed and went to comb her hair.

Dr Momin looked at Mehr and addressed her using the formal term, 'Apuni . . . You . . .'

'Don't address me so formally, as "Apuni". I am about the same age as Amina.'

Dr Momin smiled and said, 'All right. Learn a bit of nursing. You will be able to do it. You have a calm mind. And you have the physical strength for hard work.'

Amina was powdering her face. She said, 'Momin Dada, do you know what Mehr lacks the most? She loves humanity but has not been able to kindle a sense of patriotism in her mind. Not enough patriotism to be able to give her all to the country.'

Mehr responded, 'It's true. But I have learnt to love the land. Everything of mine is here. It is all merged in this land. Abbajan, Ammajan, Najma Bou, Kamal . . . This land is sacred.'

Abruptly, Amina said, 'You haven't seen this side of our motherland. Listen . . .' She began to sing in a sweet voice,

Aji Bangladesher hridoy hotey kokhon aponi
Tumi ei oporup rupey bahir holey jononi
Ogo Ma, tomay dekhey dekhey ankhi na phirey.
Tomar duar aji khuley gechhey shonar mondirey
Daan hatey tor khorgo joley, ba haatey korey shonka horon
Dui noyoney sneher hanshi, lolatnetro agun boron.
When did you come out of the heart of Bangladesh,
O my dearest Mother, with such magnificent splendour.
Mother, O Mother, my eyes are riveted on you.
The doors of your temple of gold are today unlocked.
Your right hand holds a blazing sword,
The left hand allays all fear.

Your two eyes smile with warm affection,
On your forehead, your third eye
Flames, fiery and fierce.

The memory of the image of Mahakali came to Mehr's mind. In a calm, deep and attractive voice, Dr Momin said, 'There's another image, Amina. Let me sing.

Oyi bhubon mohini
Oyi nirmal surjyo korojjol dhoroni janak jononijononi
Neel Shindhu jol dhoito chorontol
Anil bikompit shyamol anchal
Ambar chumbit bhalo himachal
Shubhro tushar kiritini.

Ah, this bewitching land,
This pure earth, bathed by a gentle sun,
Our forebears, our motherland
The blue waters of the Sindhu lap at your feet
Your emerald anchal flutters in the breeze,
Your mountains touch the sky,
A glittering white snowy diadem.

Dr Momin paused, then resumed,

Pratham pracharit tobo banabhuboney
Gyanodharmo koto kabyo kahini
Chiro kalyanomoyee tumi dhonyo
Deshey bideshey bitorichho onno
Jahnobi Jomuna, bigolito koruna,
Punyo piyush stonno bahini

From your sylvan dwelling first came out,

Knowledge, creeds, abundant stories, poems.
Always sacred, you are blessed,
You nourish the people across the world,
The sacred Ganga, molten compassion,
Your breasts provide virtuous sustenance.

Mehr could not understand the full meaning of the second song. But she could appreciate very well that for these lovers, even without songs or life, there was a deep love for the motherland in their hearts. Even if partially, the melody of the two songs and the picture they painted, planted the sapling of love for her country in her heart. She felt that the land around her was not earth, but actually, a mother. In the vast confluence at Goalondo, it really did appear that the Ganga and Jamuna rivers had combined to make a stream of milk flow from the breast of the motherland. That stream of milk was like a mother's molten mercy.

Amina twisted her hair in a bun. She said, 'Listen, Mehr. There's so much to be found in this place which you call the earth, the land. Flowers, forests, the sky. Listen, I'll sing you a song–

Kon bonetey janiney je phool gondhey emon korey akul
Kon gogoney othey re chand emon hanshi heshe
Aankhi meley tomar alo prothom amar chokh joralo
Oi alotei noyon rekhey moodbo noyon sheshey

I know not from which forest
This flower has come,
Whose fragrance maddens me so.
From which sky does the moon rise,
With this kind of a smile.
Your light beams into my eyes
As soon as them I open
And, still gazing at that light,
We'll finally close our eyes.

Do you understand? If you become a nurse here, you will be serving the motherland.'

'I have not learnt how to express my love for my country through songs and poetry. But now, I am slowly beginning to understand that the land is our mother. I shall start to learn this work whenever Momin da wants me to.'

'Come right now. Get ready along with your friend. She will be able to teach you better than I can.'

'Jah, come on!' Amina said in embarrassment. She went and stood next to Momin, ready to leave.

Mehr said, 'Let me also get ready. Just wait a bit, will you? Both of you. I shall be glad if Amina teaches me. She can educate not just me, she does that to respected doctors as well . . .'

Mehr wanted to add something more, but Amina cut in, 'Keep quiet!'

Laughing, Momin said, 'Mehr is not exactly lying.'

Amina lowered her head in embarrassment. Clapping her hands, Mehr said, 'What fun! What fun!'

Amina warned Mehr with a sharp glance. She was totally defenceless then. She, therefore, aimed the only arms left to her at Mehr.

12

Mehr began to learn nursing from Amina with a great deal of commitment and dedication. Lutfur and the khansamah were both placed in the same room. Lutfur's abdomen was operated on and stitched up again quite smoothly. The wounds in his hands and feet were still being treated. He had lost a lot of blood and was quite pale. His kidneys were deteriorating. He was in great pain as he had not been able to pass urine for several days.

On Friday, everybody had gone to offer namaz. Patients, nurses, doctors, everyone had left for prayers. But Mehr stayed back because Lutfur was in great pain. That day, the khansamah's leg was to be amputated. Dr Momin had, in the meantime, got some anaesthesia sent in from India. He had also procured those essential surgical instruments which had been lacking. The khansamah was to be taken to the Operation Theatre right after the namaz.

Lutfur had closed his eyes in pain. Sometimes, while looking at Mehr, his eyes would fill up with tears. Mehr gave him his medicines with a spoon.

He heard the azaan, the call to prayer. He listened to it with great attention. Abruptly, he called out, 'Mehr!'

Mehr asked, 'What is it?'

'This pain is unbearable. I can't even concentrate on reciting my prayers.'

'Call out to Khoda, very softly.'

Lutfur tried but failed to do as she said. His mind was crippled by his pain. He tried to lift his right hand at one point but could not. There was no blood circulation in his arms. His legs, too, were numb. His stomach was hurting agonizingly. Suddenly he said, 'Mehr!'

'Yes?'

'You had once said on the boat, "Kill me". Surely you remember that. At that time, I could not understand why somebody would want to die. Today, I want to die. I won't be able to survive this. Look, I killed people with this hand. And now it is useless. Lifeless. I have inflicted a lot of torture. Of course, I never raped a woman. Yahya Khan and Bhutto will not come to take on the load of my sins. No nation, no leader, no king will come to share this burden. This is my sin. My gunaah. Why am I not able to call out to Khoda? It is time for me to detach myself from bodily concerns. I have been dying. I will die. But what shall I say on the Day of Judgement?'

He paused, then continued, 'I know that the person who became the captain of the boat after me gave you a lot of agony. Pain. I know him. He is probably dead. But his death and Yakub's are so very different.'

He became restless in the throes of agonizing pain. Mehr remembered the doctor's advice. She tried to get him to swallow a few sleeping pills. He looked at her face and then swallowed them slowly.

Once more, he said, 'I will not survive, Mehr. I don't think Pakistan will survive either. I mean East Pakistan. When peace returns, send news of me back home. Write to them about Yakub as well. There are some dolls from Tangail in my bag. Send those too if you can. It doesn't matter if you can't.'

Even as he spoke, he fell asleep. It wasn't exactly sleep. It was more of a doze. Mehr remained staring at him for a long time. Her face was suffused with a molten compassion. For a moment she felt as though she herself was a mother, Ma Bangla. She had within her a limitless supply of kindness, love and compassion to forgive the foreign enemy.

In a little while, Dr Momin and Amina returned. The doctor examined Lutfur very minutely. Then he told Mehr, 'Stay here. There's nothing to be done now. If the medicines to make him urinate don't work today, we shall have to take some other measures tomorrow.'

Placing her hand on Mehr's back, Amina said, 'Have you heard? Habib is coming.'

Her heart began to beat faster. She asked, 'The meeting will be tomorrow, won't it?'

'Yes.'

She went towards the khansamah. Dr Momin examined him carefully for quite some time. He said, 'Riskiest operation, Amina. But it will have to be done.'

Amina looked at Momin's face, and smiled. She did not say anything. She was proud that the doctor had derived this exquisite inspiration from her. In a moment, however, she realized that this inspiration could have come from the newly acquired instruments and anaesthesia as well. For an operation to be successful, suitable equipment was what was required more than a woman's love.

Looking at Amina's face, Momin said, 'Make arrangements to bring the patient to the OT. I am going ahead.'

The doctor left. Abruptly, the khansamah looked at Mehr and said, 'Save me, Bibi Sahiba!'

Mehr did not like his mode of address. Even so, she asked, 'From whom?'

'From the doctor.'

Mehr exchanged a glance with Amina and smiled. She then said, 'Tell that to this other Bibi Sahiba. The doctor listens only to her.'

Amina had to smile. The khansamah, a simple man, folded his hands together in supplication and asked Amina, 'Bibi Sahiba, I am a poor man. What shall I do if my leg is cut off? It's better to slit my throat.'

In a mock-serious voice, Amina said, 'All right. In that case, your throat will be slit.' Amina's acting was so perfect that the khansamah took fright and said, 'Why will you slit my throat? I have been tried, you know. If I had not been wounded by that bomb, I would have been free by now.'

Amina said in an even graver voice, 'That judgement was passed in the lower court. The High Court will now take a decision.'

The khansamah grew very scared. Looking helplessly at Mehr, he said, 'Bibi Sahiba, what kind of a judgement is this!'

Mehr came up to him and placed a hand on his forehead. She said, 'Nothing of the kind is going to happen. Don't fuss. Your leg has to be cut off. There's no other way out. Otherwise, you will not be able to survive. He is a very good doctor. We cannot tell him what to do, what not to do. Don't worry. You'll be all right.'

But Amina remained serious. She kept looking at the khansamah. After a while, she went out soberly to bring in a stretcher. The khansamah asked, 'Bibi Sahiba! My leg will really have to be cut off, then?'

Mehr said, 'Yes, it will have to be cut off.'

The khansamah's eyes filled with anguish. Looking at Mehr, he said, 'We are workers. Labourers. If our leg goes, our livelihood goes. I just cannot understand why this war is taking place. When will this end? I came here straight from Patna as soon as Pakistan was created. Before that, I worked in the railways. Now I am working in the ships. That's the only difference. And now, this quarrel between the Punjabis and Bengalis. In this clash between two mighty buffaloes, we, the Biharis, are suffering. My wife and children are all in Dhaka. I don't know if they are alive or not. It's fate, Bibi Sahiba.'

Mehr said sympathetically, 'There's a war going on in our country. Fate is not favouring anyone. Not me, not you, not Lutfur. The war will stop when Bangladesh becomes independent. Our fate will be good then.'

'Our fate will be good, also? People like me, Biharis?'

'Yes, certainly, why not? Aren't the Biharis human beings as well?'

The khansamah did not reply. A deep sadness enveloped him.

Dr Momin had to fight with all his might against Death. The entire hospital became a battlefield. When the Bihari khansamah's leg was operated upon, his heartbeats suddenly grew faint. The doctor tried all kinds of remedies, but he could not bring the man's heart to normalcy again.

Gradually, the afternoon sunlight grew fainter. The Operation Theatre grew dark.

Amina had lit a lamp. The khansamah lay on a long table, unconscious. Amina held up the lamp to Dr Momin's face. The doctor decided to give an injection in the khansamah's arm.

Suddenly, Mehr ran in, to tell them about a terrible thing that had happened. Lutfur was screaming in pain. It was a terrible scream. She had placed her palm on his forehead and found him to be running an extremely high temperature. His chest was heaving hard and fast. But when she saw Dr Momin and the condition he was in, she could not tell them about this new development.

Not knowing what to do, she returned. She stood beside Lutfur's bed and looked at his face. He seemed to be sleeping peacefully. She placed her hand on his forehead. It was just a little warm.

She came out again. A few students from the Chittagong Medical College were working in the ward. Calling one of them, she asked him to examine Lutfur. The boy examined Lutfur's chest with a stethoscope. After he finished, he said, laughing, 'He's dead. You are new, so you couldn't make out that he has died.'

Mehr looked at him. Lutfur seemed to be sleeping peacefully. His eyes were closed.

The boy covered the dead body with a sheet and left. Mehr turned up the lamp that was burning by the bed and went out. Not to the camp, but to the garden. Some beautiful red roses were blooming there. Nearby were some other varieties of flowers. Bringing them in, she scattered them on Lutfur's body and offered namaz.

Later, she looked once more at Lutfur's face. Her mind flew to Lahore. She had never set eyes on Lahore. But in a house in that unseen country, a woman had been widowed today. Men fought wars, tortured others and died. Women had to suffer its consequences. This war had proven just that.

She kept the lamp back in its place, closed the door behind her and went out. The moon had risen. She went straight to the Operation Theatre. Besides Dr Momin and Amina, there were two more boys inside. Both were medical students.

One of the students asked, 'Sir, is there time to carry out a heart massage?'

Dr Momin shook his head. He said, 'If the heart was functioning all right, it would have done so by now. The man had a weak heart.'

Very carefully, Mehr went soundlessly upto Amina and whispered in her ear, 'Can you come out?'

Amina looked at Mehr, and said softly, 'Can't you see him, just look at his face . . .' She indicated Dr Momin.

Once more, Mehr whispered, 'I have something to tell you. Come on.'

Amina came out of the Operation Theatre unwillingly with Mehr. The courtyard of the temporary shed that housed the OT was beautifully moonlit. Even the shadows of their bodies seemed to be living creatures. Amina asked, 'What is it?'

'Lutfur is dead. I don't know exactly how or why it happened. He was talking about his wife. Suddenly, he began to scream . . .'

Amina had seen many deaths in the hospital. She could, therefore, find no reason for surprise in what Mehr said. She said, 'This is how people die.'

Mehr replied, 'But even then, everybody's lives are different. I am surprised that even this person, a strong Punjabi soldier, was nothing in front of Jom, the lord of death.'

Even in the midst of all this sorrow, when Amina heard the word 'Jom' on Mehr's lips, she began to laugh.

'Why are you laughing?'

'Hearing you talk about Jom. You villagers are superstitious. You are afraid even when you hear the hoot of a death owl. Death occurs within the human body. Something goes wrong in some part. If this is not cured, it becomes worse and spreads to finally reach the heart. After that, it's the end. There is no lord of death, Jom.'

Mehr asked her, 'Don't you believe in all this?'

'No.'

'In that case, how is it possible that someone survives, someone dies? Isn't it fate?'

'No.'

Abruptly, Mehr said, 'I went in a while ago to call Momin Dada. If he had seen Lutfur, maybe the man would have survived.'

Amina responded, 'All that is a misconception.'

Just then, Dr Momin came out. Amina asked, 'How is the patient, Momin Da?'

'Finished. All this effort was in vain. Mehr, how is your patient?'

Before Mehr could reply, Amina said, 'Finished. Come now, let us go to the camp. We have to eat.'

Dr Momin said, 'Not me. I'm going to my cottage. I am not hungry or thirsty.'

Piqued, Amina replied, 'I can't leave you alone. If you don't want to go to the camp, let's go to the garden. It's beautiful in the moonlight.'

Sighing, Momin said, 'All right, let's go.'

Mehr looked at them. She then said, 'Both of you go and sit there. I'll get the food ready and join you.'

Amina looked gratefully at Mehr. 'Come as fast as you can. Don't delay.'

'All right,' Mehr replied.

Amina and Momin went slowly towards the garden. The moonlight silvered their bodies brightly. Amina was wearing a beautiful, glittering blue sari. Momin was in white. To Mehr, it seemed as though she was watching a romantic scene in a film.

She went to the camp. Everything was quiet there at that time. Before she saw the battlefield and hospital, Mehr would never have believed that people could romance each other and eat keeping the dead bodies aside. In the village, a death brought grief and many days of sorrow and emotional hardship. There were all kinds of restrictions for the bereaved family, about the foods that could be eaten, about leaving the house until the last obsequies and the final ceremonies of death. Friends and relatives would visit the bereaved family to offer their condolences and to comfort them. They would try to keep the bereaved family's minds off the death. Gradually, their grief would diminish. In the battlefield or the hospital, there was no time to grieve or to express sorrow. That was the reason that the pain remained within them, eating into their minds.

It took her almost an hour to prepare the rutis, vegetables and tea. When she had finished, she put the food in a tiffin carrier, and the tea in a flask and took it to the garden. She looked around the moonlit garden, but did not see anybody. She called out, 'Amina!'

A figure came out from the shadows towards her. It was Amina. Her face was alight with laughter.

'You've brought it? Give it to me.'

She took the things from Mehr and asked, 'Are you coming or not?'

'No.'

'Why?'

'I have to cook the rice.'

The logic was not a strong one. But Amina accepted it and went back, taking the things with her. Mehr returned to the camp. Actually, Mehr had given the full dinner to Amina. After that, nobody would have any appetite for rice. The reason she had given of cooking the rice was therefore a fib. She herself ate nothing however. Lutfur's death had saddened her.

She entered the camp and lay down on her bed. Immediately, she felt at peace. Death and Love, the Grave and Flowers . . . it all seemed very natural now. Amina had brought about this sense of naturalness. She fell asleep.

Late at night, a rustling sound awoke her. She saw that Amina was changing her clothes. Instantly, she was wide awake. She could vaguely see Amina's face in the faint light of the lamp.

Hearing Mehr turn over in bed, Amina looked around at her and asked, 'Such deep sleep?'

'What's the time now?'

'It's two o'clock. Listen, Habib has arrived. He's said that you should go to meet him.'

'When?'

'I'll let you know.'

She could not go back to sleep from excitement. She asked, 'Why are you so late?'

Laughing, Amina said, 'I had to revive him again. When a patient dies, a part of him dies too. With my songs and conversation, I revive that part and keep it alive.'

'Is this medicine or love?'

Amina replied swiftly, 'It's a bit of both.' In the lamplight, Amina's face glowed like a nearby star.

Amina made no attempt to go to sleep. Mehr asked, 'Aren't you going to bed?'

'No. Where's the time? Habib has ordered that all arms and ammunition in this camp and the hospital must be shifted for the time being. Their soldiers are coming from both sides, Mymensingh and Dhaka. We shall have to leave in a short while.'

Mehr had begun to think of the hospital as her second home. She felt close to the flowers in the garden here, the graves, the hospital, the patients, the doctor, the love. It was because of Amina that she felt like this. She asked, 'So the war is not going too well for Habib and his group?'

'It's going well. Idiot! How much more can you expect from guerrilla warfare? I spoke for a long time with Habib. There's some good news.'

'What?'

'About a crore of people, refugees, have taken shelter in India. The government of that country is hard-pressed to feed them and provide them with shelter. The government will go broke if these refugees stay there for a long time. Their government has said that unless the inhuman deeds in Bangladesh stop, there is no chance of the refugees returning. And unless Sheikh Mujibur's hand is strengthened, the trouble will not stop. India will wait till winter. If this trouble does not stop by then, the army will bring back the refugees. That means war. There will be a chance of victory for the Mukti Bahini. India is now our ally. It is safe to go there.'

Mehr listened to each and every word very carefully. She said, 'I see that you know all about politics as well.'

'One has to know it. There's no other way. The time for girls to remain inside the kitchen has gone. We too should work like the men for the liberation of the country.'

'With what? What do we have?'

'With whatever we have.'

'I understand. That which you are giving Dr Momin, is that also for liberation? Or is it for yourself? Or is it because you are in love with Momin?'

Smiling, Amina said, 'I like him, and so I have fallen in love. I do not fear men. I do not fear their rules and regulations, their torture either. I love Momin. I see in him the image of a liberal-minded, upright freedom fighter. As long as I see this image, I shall love him. It is this love that will give us the strength to fight death, hopelessness, suffering.'

Mehr was astonished and amazed to hear this. She asked, 'Aren't you worried about what will happen to you? Has Momin told you that he will marry you?'

'Why should I ask him that? The weakness of girls lies in that. There is uncertainty everywhere. The lord of death is all around us, very close by. I love Momin in exactly the same way as I do those roses from the shrubs that I have planted in the garden. Neither he nor I know what will happen in the future. If he marries me, well and good. If not, fine.'

It was neither the flowers nor the graves that was the ultimate truth of this hospital. A beautiful, delicate love had also been born here. Mehr asked, 'Momin has not promised you anything?'

'No. You believe that the only kind of wedding, the real marriage, is that which is arranged by parents in a village. Kazis know the customs, but how can they know about matters of the heart? I shall have to see whether Momin's love is strong and lasting or not; whether it is just an infatuation or is it real love.'

'Will there be an element of bargaining in this? Haggling, negotiating?'

'It's not such a crude thing. It's quite sweet. Beautiful. Look, Mehr. I've noticed that you are always on your guard for no reason. You love Habib from a distance. You haven't observed him very closely. Let alone having ripened or matured fully, the love between the two of you hasn't even started.'

Mehr asked, 'But it's the same for all girls. Are you different from all other girls?'

Laughing, Amina said, 'Wah, great! You've become quite the ustaad, an expert in argument. Let me tell you something. It's always "I" at first. From that "I" comes "we". That is, the country, the world, the universe, Allah. Let the "I" become larger, bigger. Don't allow yourself to be small, to be suppressed. Stand up to the world, to men with your head held high. Let there be "shame", let there be a scandal. So what? Even the moon has a blemish. Has the moon been diminished in any way because of that?'

Suddenly, an owl called. Mehr was listening to Amina's words with amazement. How did Amina get the courage to stand up to society, to men and to customs in this way? Perhaps, it was education. Amina was highly educated. Mehr said, 'This courage only comes to girls with a high level of education.'

Amina said, 'That's not true. In every age, there are girls of this kind. For instance, Zulekha. Just look at how she bought Yusuf from the slave market? You will say that this is not the norm. That it is a deviation from conduct that is considered to be proper. But not from Zulekha's point of view. And Sonavan. Okay, I won't talk about Sonavan. She is like an Amazonian. That is, women who are like giants, demons. Actually, I don't even want to be like Zulekha. Or Sonavan. But I shall not be a slave. When Bangladesh comes into being, it won't be only for the men. It will have to be for women as well.'

It seemed to Mehr that she was listening to a speech. This oration was suitable for the Ramna Maidan in Dhaka. But the words entered every pore, every cell of her being. Till then, she had been hearing words of consolation from men. Everybody had said that Allah was the ultimate hope. But Amina was telling her something else. She was telling her to hope for Allah, and to rely on Him, but in a different way. She would have to search for Allah, and reach Allah, through her own strength and efforts. Love, war, Jihad, they all were manifestations of the inner powers within a soul.

Aachhey adi Mecca ei manob dehey
Dekhna re mon bhoye
Desh deshantor dourey ebar
Morish keno hapiye.
Mecca lies within ourselves,
My soul, don't look so with fear.

Uselessly, why do you circle the world,
And breathless, kill yourself?

She had heard this song many a time on the lips of the fakirs. But she had never understood that Allah's Mecca was present within one's own self.

She fell into a light sleep. Amina's words had filled her with hope and strength. At that point, she did not even think of Habib. She had even forgotten to think, 'I have nobody, Allah!' Instead, the thought that came to her mind, repeatedly, was 'I am. I exist. And therefore, everything exists.'

After a while, Amina woke her up. 'Get up. Have your tea. We have to bury Lutfur and the khansamah. Get some flowers. I'll take you to Habib after that. We will be leaving early in the morning. Let's pack up everything before that.'

Today, Mehr drank her tea calmly and slowly. There was no sugar in the tea. Sugar was not available anywhere. But there was cake. Amina, too, sipped her tea very slowly. Both of them were finding it difficult to leave the hospital. Only now did Mehr seem to see the camp properly. The tent was small. Two camp cots. Two leather suitcases. On the folding table was a small mirror, comb, a bottle of 'snow', a kind of face cream, hair oil and kajal. In a corner, on a small table, were the things for cooking. On a small rack were the utensils and crockery. A clothesline was strung up between two posts in the tent. Saris and blouses were hung on it. She had not noticed all these things during her time here. But today, suddenly, they had become cherished objects. They had established their own places in the camp. They had an air of permanence, as though they owned the place. Today, everything would be uprooted. Not just the camp, the entire hospital would be relocated. The garden, the operation theatre, doctors, nurses, nobody and nothing would be around. This would become the home of jackals and vultures.

They would leave, like Bedouins.

After quite a while, Amina started her chores. Seeing her, Mehr began to gather together the things around her. She had arrived here empty handed. But Amina put the clothes that Mehr had been wearing in a suitcase and said, 'This is yours.'

'But I don't have anything.'

'You have a right to these things now.'

'I shall be staying with you. What's the point of saying this is yours and that is mine?'

Amina laughed and said jokingly, 'You are going to the man of your heart. Why will you return? And also, why should he send you back? And even if he sends you back, who knows if we shall meet up again?'

Mehr blushed. She said, 'Jah, go on! I shan't be able to stay without you, I'm telling you.'

'Then you'll be digging your own grave. It won't do if you continue to have this village mindset. Understand him. Conquer yourself. This, too, is a battle. I shall dress you up as a bride today and take you to him. I shall hand you over to him and come away wiping away my tears. There won't be the music of shehnais, true, but the crickets will sing.'

'Dhet. I shan't go,' said Mehr, piqued.

'All right then, let me send word to Habib.'

'Why would you do that?'

'Because you will be going with me instead, won't you?'

'Oh, really!'

Their bantering came to an end with the appearance of Dr Momin. There was happiness on his face. In his hands was a huge bunch of roses.

'Doctor Dada, who is this huge bunch of flowers for?' asked Mehr.

'Why don't you tell me?'

'I'm not too sure. But the best one is for my friend.'

Dr Momin laughed and said, 'Yes. This bloom is for Amina. Take it.' Saying this, he gave a blood red rose to Amina. She took the flower and tucked it into the coil of her hair. Then, taking out a white rose, he handed it to Mehr, saying, 'Take this, it's for you.'

Mehr held out her hand for it and said, 'Why didn't you give me a red one?'

'This white bloom seems to match your mind, your soul. Mehr, listen! Keep your mind like a flower at all times. You will live however many days you are meant to live. You have seen many graves. Flowers are better than graves. Come now. We shall have to offer our Janaja Namaz with flowers. An elderly man is waiting for us to start.'

There was much that Mehr and Amina still had to talk about. But there was no time. The Mukti Bahini soldiers had collected the hospital's portable X-ray machine, plates, instruments, medicines, beds, cooking apparatus and carried them out on their heads. Two soldiers came to them and asked for the things that Amina had packed. Amina kept aside a suitcase. She lifted the other bundles on the men's heads. The men went away.

Dr Momin remarked, 'This must be Mehr's.'

Before Mehr could reply, Amina said, 'Yes.'

Mehr was too embarrassed to say anything.

❀

In a short while, everyone gathered together at the graveyard.

There were about a hundred graves. Dr Momin scattered the flowers and said the Janaja Namaz. All of them–the old man, Amina, Mehr, the medical students, the patients and the nurses all asked for blessings. The prayers ended in a sad, serious environment. Amina and Mehr then said goodbye and walked slowly towards the main office nearby. Dr Momin said, 'Amina, come back fast. We shall have to leave this place before nine.'

Amina responded, 'I'll be back right away.'

Mehr felt a great emptiness in her heart. On the way, she said, 'I had stopped thinking about everything after meeting you. I wonder when we will meet again?'

'Come to the Garo Hills after this. I shall wait for you.' Amina paused, then continued, 'Never forget that I am your friend. Don't be sad. You have strength and power within you. Take Allah's name. Take Ma Bangla's name. You will find everything in them.'

Mehr hugged Amina and remained in her embrace quietly for a while. 'You know, Amina, I am still afraid,' she said at last.

'Don't be afraid. Don't feel inferior to anybody. Come on, now.'

Amina disengaged herself from Mehr and wiped away her tears.

Mehr said, 'Let me know when you get married.'

Laughing, Amina replied, 'I am not thinking as far ahead as you are. Let us first overcome this situation . . .'

They saw the camp ahead of them.

13

After leaving Mehr with Habib, Amina turned back.

Habib was sitting in the tent. However, the tents nearby were all empty. He was talking with another person. Seeing Mehr, he quickly finished his conversation and sent him off. He looked at Mehr and said, 'You are all right now, aren't you? You are looking really well. Sit.'

Mehr did not sit down. She stared at Habib. She said, 'You are not looking too good yourself. Are you going through a lot of hardship?'

She sat down on a bundle. Looking at Habib's darkened face, sunken eyes, dry and rough hair which had not been oiled for a long time, his sleeveless vest, lungi and his parched lips, she sighed.

Inside the forest, the light was weak. There were mosquitoes even during the day. There were a few bunkers nearby.

Habib asked, 'Did you ask for me? Why?'

Smiling, Mehr said, 'Shall I have to tell you even if you the reason? We haven't met for a long time. A lot of things have happened. Don't we want to talk, and listen to each other, to our hearts' content?'

Abruptly, feeling vexed, she said, 'When we came from the boat, I was in a state of shock. I was ashamed and completely dispirited. And yet you never came to see me at Bhuyanpur?'

Lighting up a cigarette, Habib sat on another bundle and said, 'There was just no time then. The arms and ammunition that we had captured had to be despatched here secretly and to the Garo Hills. Right afterwards, the Khan soldiers came at us from three sides. They troubled us for almost ten hours. But I had seen you on the boat . . .'

'Really?'

'Ismail and I were fishing on the river bank. We had been observing the fleet for some time. Several times in the past few days, we had crossed and re-crossed your boat. I knew about your capture. I knew about the old man's wife who had been imprisoned as well. Because of this, our determination grew stronger. In the meantime, Lutfur was also captured by our men. He also gave me news about you . . .'

Mehr vaguely remembered, as in a dream, the two men with fishing rods who had been sitting on the river bank. 'I saw those two men with the fishing rods, but I couldn't recognize them.'

'What would have been the point of disguising ourselves if we could be recognized? It's not enough just to wish to meet you. There should also be time for it. Where was the time?'

'You could have sent a letter, some news, you know.'

'I could have. I did not think of it, that's true.'

'I am ruined! Not once did you think about that!' Mehr still looked upset.

Smiling, Habib drew on his cigarette. He then came near her and said, 'Where? Nothing has happened. I see nothing wrong with you. You are the brimming Jamuna herself.'

Habib said this very naturally. Mehr was satisfied. She understood that he did not wish to recall unpleasant matters. She said, 'I don't want to talk about these things. I feel disgusted when I remember it.'

Habib said impatiently, 'Forget all that now, Mehr. I knew you since you were a little girl. Death is chasing me everywhere. It's only luck that I'm not dead yet. This time, though, it's uncertain. They have surrounded us on three sides. I don't know if Momin and the others will reach safely.'

Mehr wanted to say something, but just then, a sabre jet roared overhead. They could hear the jet circling above them. Habib said calmly, 'They are now looking around for an opportunity. Any day now, they will attack this forest. We shall have to fight them here. But it is difficult to fight them face-to-face. They have camped at Chandpur village, about a mile from here. There they . . .'

Mehr asked, 'Why did you send away the hospital from here?'

'This coming battle is probably going to be a very big one. That is why the central office has also been shifted from here. They will attack the villages once the rains are over. We should be prepared.'

Puffing on his cigarette, Habib looked at Mehr. There was a great deal of pleasure on his face. Laughing, Mehr asked, 'What are you looking at?'

'I'm looking at you. Do you know what you look like now?'

'What?'

'Like gold that has been polished by fire.'

Mehr, understanding his meaning, blushed. Happily, she said, 'I know you will never leave me.'

Habib smoked his cigarette very slowly, then said, 'That is how I am. I cannot leave, I cannot let go. I've met many girls. But nobody could take me away from you. I've seen many countries as well. But I haven't seen any country which I could love as much as Bangladesh. Now I know every blade of grass, every leaf of this country. There's just one thing that I love which I have sacrificed. That is Pakistan.'

'When will Bangladesh come into being?'

'I don't know. We have a Bahini, an army. But we don't have enough arms. We have asked for India's help. If this happens, Bangladesh will come into being quite soon. If not, we shall have to fight for a long time. Like the Vietnamese.'

Mehr looked at Habib's face. She paused, wordless. It seemed to her that she was listening to those famous heroes that she had read about in her textbooks. She had heard her father speak about Hyder Ali, Tipu Sultan, Siraj-ud-Daulah. They had all died fighting. She said, 'Do you know how I feel when I hear you say these things?'

'How?'

'As though I am studying History once again at school in Kalihati.'

'Really?'

'Yes.'

'I am not such a great warrior. But our war is a great one.'

'Will you win?'

'Don't ask me that. We shall have to win. There is no other way out now.'

Mehr suddenly remembered Yakub. She asked, 'Did you know Yakub?'

'Yes. Lutfur told me everything. Both of them have gone. Towards the end, Lutfur also understood that Pakistan will not remain intact.'

Mehr wished to say something, but there was a sudden roar of cannons. Alarmed, Mehr got up and went near Habib. He drew her close to him in an embrace and said, 'They are shelling us. It's time for me to start our preparations. Come, let's go to the bunker.'

The roar of cannons continued for a while. Mehr put her head on Habib's chest and gradually calmed down. She could hear the sound of Habib's heartbeats. He lifted up her face and kissed her with deep affection. Immediately, Mehr felt much more confident.

Habib said, 'Come, let's go. Any delay will be dangerous.'

Both of them entered a bunker a little distance away. Once more, there was the roar of cannons.

There was a field telephone inside the bunker. Habib lifted it and listened. He then said, 'Excellent. Fire from the opposite side of the cannon. Try to silence it. Get ready for the attack at night.' After a pause, Habib continued, 'How many LMGs do we have? Two? Good. Don't leave the bunker. Keep firing till evening. Understand?'

After another pause, Habib said, 'There aren't many people here. We shall leave in the evening. How many are they? A platoon. Will you be able to take them on? Excellent. What did you say the weather is going to be like? Rainy? Windy also? Excellent.'

Habib put down the receiver and looked at Mehr. She was examining the bunker minutely. It was a very large space. There were racks of files along the walls. There were four LMGs in the four sides of the bunker. Four people manned them. Through an aperture that was camouflaged from outside, they were looking at the distance through binoculars.

Habib sat down on a folding chair that rested on the wall. He asked the men, 'What do you see?'

'The camp. We can see that clearly. The Khans have camped at the school in Chandpur village. We can see a tank.'

'Okay.'

The others did not say anything.

Habib said, 'Mehr.'

'What?'

The roar of the cannons stopped even as he began to speak. Once more, the telephone rang. Habib asked, 'It's disabled? Okay, okay. Continue.'

He put the receiver down. Both of them came up from the bunker. On reaching the tent, Habib said, 'Sit down. They'll be bringing in food. We'll be able to talk for a long time today. There is a chance of rain. It's most likely that they will not attack. Still, it's difficult to say. We shall be attacking them at night. I'll send you off by boat.'

'You won't be going?'

'No.'

'Tell me, what's been happening back in your home?'

'My home?' Habib's face became very sorrowful. 'They have captured Abbajan, Ammajan, everybody.'

It was the same everywhere. Sameer, Ismail, Amina, everybody . . .

'There are guerrillas everywhere. They are keeping the guerrillas and the people of the Awami League under strict observation.'

After a pause, Mehr asked, 'Are you inconvenienced if I stay with you?'

'No. You cannot stay.'

'Why?'

'I don't want you to. We need only soldiers here.'

'The times are such, who knows what will happen? If I am to die, I'll die with you.'

'Do you want to be a sati? Sacrificing yourself along with me?' Habib began to laugh.

'No. I want to be Sita. I am enjoying this exile.'

'The *Ramayan* is over, done with. Ravan has kidnapped Sita. She has even been rescued from the Ashok garden. Why the exile now?'

'Ram has not got back his kingdom yet. You can say, instead, that Sita has been sacrificed. Banished.'

Habib began to laugh uproariously. After a while, he said, 'Ram banished Sita after listening to what others were saying. I have not done any such thing, have I?'

Mehr said, 'You did abandon me for a while, didn't you? You didn't even try to find out anything about my condition.'

'That's true.'

'I can't bear to be separated now. I want to stay with you and serve Bangladesh and you.'

'You will be able to render this service in the hospital.'

With a sad mind, Mehr said, 'You know, I get all kinds of doubts and fears. When will our nikah take place . . .'

'Leave those thoughts aside . . .'

'Why?'

'It may not happen. At least, let this war be over.'

Mehr's mind trembled at the expectation of some unspecified accident of some kind. She asked, 'I shall always pray to Allah for you. Tell me something. How much do you love me?'

Habib replied, 'I don't know. But let me tell you something. The terrible things that happened to you after I left you made me really sad. I also felt a great deal of disgust. Men never wish to marry a girl to whom such a thing has happened. From time immemorial, this evil tradition has found a place in the minds of men. Nobody will blame me even if I abandon you. But I have thought about it and I have overcome that evil custom. In any case, I can't do such a thing. Many Bangla girls are in this condition. Some have babies in their wombs. What will happen to them? Unlike Ram, I cannot sacrifice Sita after listening to gossip about her impurity. Ram was a contemptible coward. It is only possible to be Ramchandra in a Hindu society. The social setup of Bangladesh will have to be altered.' Habib paused and then continued in a very soft voice, 'I did not wish to say these things today. But you compelled me to say them. I love you. But I cannot speak in the way they do in films and in theatres. Of course there will be no nikah as long as there is war. The wedding will take place when Bangladesh is liberated. If I remain alive.'

Mehr was moved by Habib's words. She came close to him and said, 'You are a divine being. I came as fast as I could to you just to hear you say these things. I had sent word through the old man . . .'

'That old man is a very good person. He has a great deal of affection for you.' Habib took one of Mehr's hands in his own and asked, 'So, tell me, Mehr, who gave you these conch-shell bangles?'

'Sameer.'

'Sameer? Why?'

'Some refugee had left them behind in the sands of the Jamuna while fleeing. This pair of bangles and two dolls–a bride and a bridegroom. He said to me, "Baideo, I am giving you these bangles." He calls me Baideo, elder sister.'

'Sameer is a very good man.'

Mehr said, 'His home is in Dhaka. He has not heard from anybody after 25th of March. His elder sister, his parents . . . nobody. When he gave me these bangles, he was extremely worried and anguished, remembering his sister.'

'There's no need for so many explanations, Mehr. I know. He is as innocent as a child. I have seen him taking out the bride and bridegroom dolls sometimes, in his free time. He stares at them, forgetting everything else. He gave you these bangles on an impulse. It does not have much significance.'

Mehr's mind was clear now. After meeting Habib, she felt as though she had got everything. Habib gently fondled her hand and then drew her close. Mehr felt an inexpressible peace and joy.

That sense of peace and contentment overwhelmed her till evening. But gradually, Habib began to get ready for battle. In the meantime, the old man had appeared. Putting Mehr in the old man's care, Habib took his soldiers and went to the battlefield.

Mehr went with the old man to the temporary and secret landing ghat of the Banar river and climbed onto a boat carrying arms and ammunition. Once on the boat, she curled up and went to sleep. She was immersed in her dream world even then.

The old man sat on the tin roof and sang a bhatiali song. It was a new one, different from the traditional type:

Mukti Foujey daakey morey
Thakum kemney kow

The Freedom fighters call out to me
Tell me, how can I remain behind...

With her eyes closed, Mehr dreamt of war. With an LMG on his shoulder, Habib was walking through the forests to attack the Pakistani soldiers' camp in Chandpur. Not just Habib, countless soldiers of Bangladesh were busy at that task.

Next day, they alighted at the Narundi ghat. With their belongings, they crossed the railway lines and moved through the villages until they came once more to the Brahmaputra. Travelling onwards, one day, they reached Mancachar. From there, she came to

Phulbari. For the last ten days, she had been working temporarily in the camp. She had not got any news of the hospital. She was eagerly waiting for some news asking her to go to the hospital.

Mehr had been totally engrossed in relating the story of her life. While she had been talking, I had noticed that her personality had been imbued with the characteristics of her rural life. But gradually, through the consciousness of a wider national power, she had acquired a new self-confidence. Through her descriptions, an unfamiliar side of the amazing liberation struggle of Bangladesh came vividly to life. So far, we had only read about the terrible conditions and hopelessness of the women who had been raped in the newspapers. But now, after hearing all this with my own ears, I realized that it was all very wretched and touching at the same time. It seemed that I had heard the story of a sister's life from her own mouth.

It was only after looking through the windows that I realized that the evening sunlight had gradually descended on Phulbari. It was as though we had traversed the battlefield to arrive at this peaceful state. Before our eyes was, it seemed, a cinema screen. Blatant torture, silent grief, armed battle, and enveloped by these, only graves. On top of the graves were flowers. The stories of Yakub, Lutfur, Habib, Najma kept coming to me, clouding my mind. But at the conclusion of all these stories, this girl stood here before us in the flesh.

While Mehr had been speaking, Bagaitkar had been noting down what she said in a notebook that he carried. Mehr asked him, 'Do you know what happened to Malobika? I could not meet her. She was taken to Ranchi.'

Mehr sighed. Momentarily, we were all silent. Then once again, Mehr said, 'I have no news of her. I hear there's a very big hospital there. I always pray for her before Allah.'

Bagaitkar said, 'I too am praying to Ishwar. I have heard many other stories like what you have told me about Malobika. This happened to many girls in Dhaka on the 25th of March. Sameer's sister must also be in the same condition as Malobika. It's the same story everywhere. This torture, this inhuman brutalization of women is rare in the history of the entire world.'

I said, 'That's true. Even in Assam, a long time ago, the Burmese had tyrannized the land. From what I hear, the Nazis did the same thing in Europe. But what Yahya Khan has done has surpassed them all.'

Mehr said, 'It will be a gunah to allow this torture and tyranny to go on further. Habib and his companions are fighting, but they need arms.'

Bagaitkar said, 'I know they need arms. We have to do all we can to free Bangladesh. Otherwise, what will happen to the lakhs of refugees?'

Bagaitkar was finding it difficult to write in the darkening light. Noticing this, Mehr said, 'I'll go and bring a lamp. It's been a while since you had your lunch. What do you say to some tea?'

Bagaitkar said, 'Oh yes. I had forgotten all about my stomach.'

Mehr left the room. I asked Bagaitkar, 'What do you think of Yakub?'

'Yakub is their conscience.'

'You're right. And Habib?'

'A free man. Unbound, unrestricted.'

I wanted to ask him more, but Mehr returned with a lamp. Keeping it on the table, she said, 'You'll be having some snacks won't you? There are no provisions inside. There's only bananas and some pineapples. Will that do?'

'Yes,' said Bagaitkar, and added a question, 'There's no sign of Pulin Babu?'

Mehr's face clouded with worry. She said, 'There must be some problem for sure. Otherwise, why should he be so late? These days, the Pakistani soldiers have been carrying out all kinds of atrocities in the Mymensingh-Tangail-Rongpur region. Habib had said he would be coming here. He has not been able to.' The worry lines on her forehead became pronounced.

Bagaitkar smiled, and said, 'There's no point worrying. Instead, let's go ahead to Mancachar. What do you say?'

'Not a bad idea,' she replied.

After having our tea, we got ready to leave. Mehr locked the door. I went ahead to call the Jeep. I had just reached the end of the alley when I saw that another Jeep had come to a halt there. Pulin Babu got down in an agitated frame of mind.

Not noticing me in the dark, he almost bumped into me. I caught him with both hands and asked, 'Is something the matter, Pulin Babu? You seem very disturbed.'

Pulin Babu was a middle-aged man. Short. Seeing me, he said, 'You have been waiting?'

Jokingly, I said, 'Ours not to ask why. Ours but to do and die. We are just following your orders.'

There was no answering smile on Pulin Babu's long face, as there would have been on other days. He said, 'Robin Babu, this is no time for jokes. It's good that you are still here. We shall have to leave right now for Tura, and then, from Tura to Dalu.'

'So we shall have to go beyond Tura?'

'Yes. Where is Bagaitkar?'

Even as he spoke, Bagaitkar and Mehr arrived. Anxiously, Mehr asked, 'Pulin da, why are you so late?'

'Don't ask! Many of our boys are dead. The dead bodies have been carried by boat to Mancachar. The refugees are agitated. People are dying in this war of liberation. On the other hand, in the camps there is an outbreak of cholera, chickenpox and gastroenteritis. Bagaitkar! You have vaccines and Mexaform with you, don't you? Give two bags to the driver. Let him go on ahead.'

Bagaitkar obeyed the orders silently. He took Pulin Babu's vehicle and went on a little way ahead. It stopped near our vehicle in front of the hotel.

Pulin Babu asked, 'Mehr, have you got any news of the other side?'

'No.'

'The news is not good. The freedom fighters are putting up a huge fight, very near Mancachar. A regiment of Khan soldiers is heading towards Dalu. They are just across the border now. There's been a huge attack on Madhuban.'

'Have you got news of Habib?'

'No. I've got news of Amina, though.'

'Where is she?'

Pulin Babu said, 'Let's go to our vehicle.'

Mehr asked impatiently, 'Where is Amina now?'

Pulin Babu said abruptly, 'I find it very difficult to describe these events, Mehr. Let me tell you in brief that if you had gone with them that day, you would never have reached this side. All of them fell into the hands of the Razakars and Al Badr forces. There was a huge battle. Dr Momin died on the spot. Amina had a gun. She fought for a long time. In the end, she got a bullet in the chest. She died right there. We've lost everything. Portable X-ray machines, surgical instruments, medicines, nurses, doctors–nobody and nothing is left. There was a regiment of Pakistani soldiers with the Razakars, the Internal Security Force. That's why this happened.'

Mehr could not believe what she had heard. Amina was Life itself. Laughter, song, responsibility, self-confidence, fearlessness–she was a symbol of all of this. She asked, 'Has her body been found?'

'Yes. They were attacked in a Hajong village near Haluaghat. I can't remember the name. They were right near the border when they were suddenly attacked. They found Dr Momin in a half-dead condition and killed him. But they could not do that to Amina. The Hajong villagers said that they had never thought that a woman could fire a gun in this way. They died, but because they had fought back, they were not captured. The attackers had surrounded the village. Nobody could escape.'

The three of us moved forward through Phulbari's dark and silent streets towards the hotel. Suddenly, I realized that Mehr had slumped down against me. I caught her. I told Pulin Babu, 'Pulin Babu, please stop describing these events.'

Pulin Babu looked at Mehr. He was contrite and regretted what he had said. He said to her, 'Mehr. You cannot fight for freedom with such a weak heart. It's not just you. Many girls of Bangladesh have lost everything. Amina was a valorous woman. She was like the Rani of Jhansi, like Begum Zeenat Mahal, like Joan of Arc. She died fighting. Not only had she lost everything, she also gave her life for the freedom of her country.'

Mehr raised her head from where it rested on me. We had in the meantime reached our Jeep. She caught hold of the Jeep and somehow managed to stand normally. She looked at Pulin Babu and said, 'I stand defeated before her. Laughter was her life. Her laughter has gone. She has not gone alone. She's taken Dr Momin with her.'

Pulin Babu said, 'This is what you should say. "Amina has done what she had to do. Now it's my turn to work." Now come along. We'll have to hurry.'

Bagaitkar had in the meantime finished his task. We sat in the Jeep as soon as the driver came back. We took leave of Sheal. Pulin Babu asked Mehr and me to sit in front. He sat with Bagaitkar at the back. Within about five minutes, we left Phulbari and came to the hill road to Tura. Mehr gasped frequently as the Jeep went on the uneven roads. Her chest heaved. I noticed her eyes, still and blank.

Standing indifferently on the sides of the road were hundreds, thousands of trees. The ground underneath them could not be seen. Long ago, I had come this way to the Bangrim valley with a very well-known archaeologist. I had seen the relics of the lives and the last remains of the people of an ancient era then.

On the banks of a small stream were scattered countless pebbles. The archaeologist had picked up some of them and said, 'Perhaps the skeleton of a pre-historic man is hidden right here.' This was not at all surprising. People have lived for millions of years on these hills. For thousands of years, people have lived in the Brahmaputra valley and in the valley of the Padma-Jamuna downstream. Actually, people are never destroyed. People have always had to struggle to survive. Mehr was the enduring emblem of one of these struggles.

At one point, I saw a beautiful deer standing unconcerned in the middle of the road. Its eyes shone darkly. The driver stopped the car. He said, 'Babu, if only we had a gun!'

Mehr looked angrily at the driver and said, 'You only think of killing, of eating. Will you ever be able to create a creature like this? Just look how beautiful it is!'

The driver looked at Mehr in astonishment. She was not looking at him. She stared at the innocent, dumb, beautiful deer. Abruptly, she turned to me and said, 'Dada, I feel as though I'm looking at Amina!'

I understood that the deer really was Amina. It was a symbol of a sweet and wordless beauty.

At the back, Pulin Babu and Bagaitkar were sound asleep. The deer kept gazing at us. Mehr could not tear her eyes away from it. The driver, not knowing what else to do, switched off the engine.

14

The beauty of Tura is beyond description. But when we entered the city at about two at night, it looked like a graveyard. The lights appeared to be sentinels of that graveyard. But we seemed to find life even within that graveyard.

We went to wake up Bhowmik. He was already up and talking to someone. Seeing him awake at two in the morning, I asked him, 'Does your shop remain open through the night?'

'Yes. There's no such thing as night or day for me, you know, Robin Babu. This is like an Information Centre of Bangladesh. Where are you coming from? Where are you going?'

I had left Pulin Babu and the others outside. When I called him aside and explained the purpose of our visit to him, he said, 'Look Robin Babu, we shall have to call up beforehand. You will get all the information here. I am in touch with the camps.'

Bhowmik took me to the telephone room. He said, 'I will not be able to take you there. But I can get some people from there to come here.'

I said, 'Actually, it's Pulin Babu who will know exactly whom to talk with.'

As soon as he heard Pulin Babu's name, Bhowmik was full of respect. 'Pulin Babu of Bangladesh? We are from the same place. Okay, please call him.'

Pulin Babu, Mehr and Bagaitkar had in the meantime alighted from the Jeep and came into the shop. I took Pulin Babu into the room with the phone. Bagaitkar and Mehr sat in the outer room.

Once the connection to Headquarters came through, Pulin Babu spoke for quite some time on the phone. After putting the receiver down, he called for me. 'Robin Babu!'

'Yes?'

'We shall have to leave immediately.'

'Yes, all right. But who will show us the way?'

Pulin Babu replied, 'We have to go by the Dalu road. Their people will give us a signal on the way. You know that road, don't you?'

Bhowmik said, 'Robin Babu knows the Garo Hills very thoroughly. I know him since the time his brother was living here. I am sure you have not had dinner in Phulbari. I'll make some arrangements for tea. Have it before going.'

Pulin Babu and I looked at each other. Pulin Babu asked, 'How long will it take?'

'Not long. Ten minutes.'

I looked at the hospitable Bhowmik. On his face was a happy smile, in his eyes a boundless sweetness. He was untiring and had a limitless capacity for work. The short, darkish man looked the same since I had last met him. He was prepared to satisfy the workers of the liberation struggle of Bangladesh in the same way that he satisfied the buyers who came to his shop. His family had originally come from Chittagong. He still had relatives there. Quite a few of them had come here as refugees.

Pulin Babu went outside. Bhowmik asked me all kinds of questions. He then went to make arrangements for tea. I sat alone, quietly, in his shop for about five minutes. Only the electric light lit up the room.

For the first time, I realized that the people of the valley were linked to the Bangladesh libertion struggle in two ways. These were in the areas of war and of supply. We had to give everything we could to the fighters, from arms and ammunition to emotional support, love and affection. I was disgusted at myself for having neglected this responsibility for so long. If Bagaitkar had not come, and if I had not got inspiration from my wife, I would probably not have come here at all. And if I had not come here, I would probably not have known about this matchless, unique struggle.

After about eight minutes or so, the tea and biscuits arrived. Bhowmik ushered in Bagaitkar and the others. The four of us sat down and drank the hot tea. Bhowmik took some tea and biscuits to our driver outside. He took out some supari, dried betel nuts, from a corner of the shop and cut them up into pieces with a cutter. Taking some paan, he prepared paan-supari for us and offered them to us on a plate. Looking at Mehr, he asked, 'What did you say your name was?'

'Mehrunnisa.'

'You are from Kalihati, aren't you?'

'Yes. How did you know?' Mehr was surprised.

'An old man had come here and made enquiries. He tried to call Phulbari. But he couldn't get through.'

'When did he come?' asked Mehr.

'This morning.'

'Where is he now?' asked Mehr.

'He's gone to the camp at Dalu. I'm not sure exactly where.'

Mehr did not ask any more questions. I asked her, 'Who do you think it was, Mehr?'

Smiling, Mehr replied, 'It can't be anybody else but Dada from Islampur. Who would want to know about me except him?'

Bhowmik said, 'Yes. He was from Islampur. The old man has lost everything. Wife, children, house, property . . .'

But the fact was that this kind of thing that had happened to so many Bangladeshis did not seem to disturb anybody. Everybody had learned to bear it. Some tried to avenge this. Others just bore it even as time passed because they were powerless to do anything.

After having the tea and paan, we got ready to leave. Bhowmik came up to the vehicle to see us off. He folded his hands as he bid us goodbye. He touched Pulin Babu's feet and said, 'I have not seen our old homestead since 1947. If, by your grace, I get to see it again, I shall die happy.'

We were all in the Jeep by then. Mehr and I sat in the front seat as before. We, too, bid farewell to Bhowmik. The driver started the vehicle.

It was almost three o' clock. From Bhowmik's shop, our Jeep sped to the marketplace. From there, it took a left turn and went on a twisting path to a petrol pump. After filling up with petrol, we took the road to the east and began our journey to Dalu.

After a while, we reached a checkpost. After crossing that, we continued on the road to Dalu, buffeted by the strong currents of the cold, late night wind.

Mehr said, 'This is a dry area. There is no large river here.'

I asked, 'Do you love your country?'

'Very much.'

'Let the country become free. I'll visit it one day.'

Mehr laughed. 'Are you waiting for the time when you will be welcomed like a son-in-law? We need people, manpower now. Fighters. India is such a huge country. If they wish to help . . . quickly . . .'

She smiled and left her sentence unfinished.

I said, 'India will help when the time is right.'

'When will the time be right? After all of us are dead and gone?'

'How can I say when the right time will come?'

Mehr said, 'How much longer before it is the right time? It's already the right time.'

I did not know much about politics or warfare. Even so, I felt that Mehr was speaking the truth. It was time that India took some action.

Our Jeep picked up speed. I kept an alert eye on the warning signs by the roadside. I did not speak to Mehr for a while. Bagaitkar was asleep. I told the driver to stop the vehicle when he saw some kind of signal or a sign.

We moved on in silence for a while. The wind grew very strong. Mehr wrapped the anchal, the free end of her sari, around her head like a scarf to protect herself from the wind. Even though I was busy looking for a sign on the road so that I would not miss the way to our destination, I did not let go of any excuse for levity even at this moment. I said, 'You look very good with the oroni around your head. You will look very beautiful dressed as a bride. Let me know when you get married.'

Mehr answered in a very sweet voice, 'Dada, whom shall I invite to my wedding if not you? Will you really come?'

'Why do you feel that I won't come?'

'No, I don't get that feeling. But when I see you, I do feel as though you are a little helpless, a little disturbed when you are away from Bou,' she said, referring to Maloti as her elder sister-in-law.

'Dhet! Are you joking? Are you mocking me? Tell me the truth.'

'I'm not mocking you. You look as though you don't have much strength to bear sorrow.'

'You're just guessing.'

While talking playfully with Mehr, an easy relationship had grown between us. Talking to each other had warmed us up a bit. We would have talked some more, but the driver stopped the vehicle at that point. The headlight shone on an old man in a lungi. The man came forward.

But instead of speaking to me, he looked at Mehr and said straightaway, 'Mehr, come down. Turn the Jeep around and park it inside the forest here. We shall have to walk to the camp.'

I woke up Pulin Babu and Bagaitkar. Hastily, they got down from the vehicle.

Mehr and the old man went ahead, talking to each other. Pulin Babu, Bagaitkar and I followed. Two or three people were standing there. Bagaitkar said to them, 'There are bags of medicines and other things in the Jeep. They need to be taken out and brought along with us.'

One of them said, 'It will be better if the vehicle itself is brought in.'

'Whatever you think is best.'

I saw many tents. Most of them were lit up with small lamps. Some were in darkness. Mehr's Dadajan took us to a large tent that was situated right at the end and left us there. These tents had been set up in a portion of deep forest that had been cleared. The place was isolated and full of wild animals.

As soon as we entered, a young man came forward and took us to a small table around which some chairs were arranged. He requested us to sit there. When we were seated, an officer of the Eastern Rifles and a well-built Punjabi came in. After introductions were over, Pulin Babu told them about the materials that Bagaitkar had brought. The two men listened quietly, then took an inventory of the materials that had been brought, in the meantime, to the camp. The Punjabi examined them minutely. He then looked at Bagaitkar and said, 'These boots will be useful. The freedom fighters are facing great difficulties because of their footwear. Many thanks to the people of Maharashtra!'

Pulin Babu enquired about how the war was going. He asked, 'Is it true that the Pakistanis have totally destroyed the hospital and all that was in it in the Haluaghat area?'

'It's true,' said the elderly man. 'We could not save them. They were surrounded and attacked while they were resting in the village. Everyone was killed.'

Pointing to Mehr, Pulin Babu said, 'Perhaps you recognize her. Amina's friend. She learnt nursing under Dr Momin for some time.'

The man looked closely at Mehr, then said, 'Your friend died fighting. We are all very saddened by this, but we are also awestruck by her valour. Habib himself had gone with his fighters to save them. But he could not reach in time.'

Mehr asked abruptly, 'Where is Habib now?'

'He was here. For the past four days, he was in action. We are expecting him to return today. You know Habib?'

'Yes, we are from the same village.'

Mehr was about to add something else, but no words came from her mouth. To save her from embarrassment, nobody asked her anything else.

'How many soldiers do you have with you?' asked Bagaitkar.

The man smiled, but did not reply immediately. After a pause, he said, 'We have trained many youths. But we have no weapons, no ammunition. It will be a great thing if your government helps. What do you say, Sardarji!'

The Punjabi also laughed. He said, 'All these decisions are for those above to make.'

The other person said, 'Bagaitkarji. We accept the material you have brought as a gift from your country. It's very late. It's best that you go to sleep now.'

There was no emotion, sorrow or despair in their words. Each one of them had a calm sense of responsibility.

We left Pulin Babu with them, talking and discussing about matters. The three of us proceeded to a tent. It was a small one, but strong. It was lit up by four or five candles. There were three camp cots. Each one had a blanket as well. Without further delay, we lay down.

Bagaitkar and Mehr took the beds on the sides. I climbed onto the middle one. But for a long time, I could not sleep. Bagaitkar, however, began to snore as soon as he lay down. I could make out from the sound of her tossing and turning that Mehr, too, was unable to sleep. Sleep had vanished from my eyes. I lay motionless. In the meantime, the candles went out. From outside, a cool breeze came and caressed our faces. The chirping of the sleepless birds could be heard outside. I looked repeatedly towards Mehr but could not see anything. Everything was in darkness.

After a while, it began to rain. Mehr's tossing and turning increased. I listened to the cadence of the unceasing rain. After a while, I gradually realized that Mehr was keening in distress like an animal. Hearing that, I called out to her, 'Mehr!'

She replied, 'Dada, are you not able to sleep?'

'No.'

'I can't sleep either.'

'Why are you keening like this? Crying?'

'It's always like this when I try to sleep. It's more today. All kinds of thoughts have been coming to my mind. I am remembering Amina . . .'

'Try and get some sleep now. It's time to rest.'

Both of us became quiet. The sound of rain grew louder. Gradually, my eyes closed.

When I woke up the next day, neither Bagaitkar nor Mehr were in their beds. The rosy morning light lit up the red, earthen floor. I lay in bed for a while. There was no sign of anybody around. However, I could not remain like that for too long. I got up, and rubbing my eyes, went outside.

There was nobody outside the tent either. But there was a crowd of people outside a large tent some distance away. I searched for and found some water. I took out my toothpaste, cleaned my teeth and washed my face. I then proceeded slowly to the tent.

On the left, some distance away, I saw some men on the parade ground exercising. The Punjabi man was inspecting them. He was shouting out some commands. In all likelihood, some kind of training was going on there. To the right, in another tent, lay some arms and ammunition. A freedom fighter stood guard with a rifle. To the side of that tent was the path we had taken last night. It was a path that could easily be negotiated by a Jeep. I saw our own vehicle waiting nearby. Seeing me, the driver called out. As soon as I reached the Jeep, he whispered in my ear, 'Babu, you were asleep. I don't know, maybe we shall have to leave immediately.'

'If we have to leave, I will . . .'

'In that case, get ready.'

I looked at the tent in front of which people were crowding around. I asked, 'What's happening there?'

'Some wounded soldiers were brought in at night. One of them is very seriously wounded. Bagaitkar ji says that we shall have to take him to Gauhati to be operated on.'

I shivered.

Slowly, I went towards the crowd. Looking closely, I saw that some people were bandaging the eyes of a tall, well built man. There were several bandages on his body. Mehr was looking on. Bagaitkar and Pulin Babu were standing away from the crowd, along with the elderly man we had met yesterday. They were talking in whispers with each other very seriously.

I called out, 'Mehr.'

Everybody turned around and looked at me, including Mehr. But as soon as her gaze fell on me, tears began to flow freely from her eyes. I wanted to beckon her to come closer. But at that point, Bagaitkar indicated through his eyes that I should not do that. Instead, he came forward and taking me by the hand, brought me out, away from the crowd, to the open space outside.

I asked, anxiously, 'Who is he?'

Bagaitkar replied in a very serious tone, 'Habib. We will take him back with us to Gauhati. We will go with him in an ambulance. Mehr will come with us. She won't be going to Phulbari now.'

There was no need to say anything else. I could visualize the entire incident clearly. I understood why Mehr's eyes had filled with tears when she looked at me.

Bagaitkar said, 'Come, let's have tea. We'll leave as soon as the ambulance arrives.' With this, he took me with him to the first tent that we had gone to last night.

'Has he lost his eyesight?' I asked.

'Probably. He's very seriously wounded.'

❀

We came by the Krishnai road on our return journey. It was better than the other road, but it had more bends and was not asphalted. The weather was clear. Gradually, the sun came up. The ambulance followed us as though it was a small white mobile house. The protagonist of my story and I sat as before on the front seat. The battlefield seemed very far away.

Within my lifespan, my country had been involved in three wars. All three had stopped at Assam's borders. The Japanese had come and returned from Kohima. The Chinese turned back from near Bhalokpong during the 1962 war. The war of 1965 did not come to Assam at all. There was little chance of this war of 1971 coming right into Assam either.

Only refugees and wounded soldiers came to our peaceful valley. No doubt, today, the people of Assam were disturbed. But we witnessed the war as distant spectators. We were like the blind Dhritarashtra. We did not have supernatural vision. The modern Sanjayas described Kurukshetra in various ways, but we could not even do that. We just listened. Sitting at home, we discussed what was good, what was bad. We watched the contours of the war. We sighed when we saw refugees. We were sorrowful when we saw the wounded. We were perturbed with the price rise. Our experience of war was an indirect one. It was a distant thing. Even in the descriptions that I have given, there are no first-hand experiences. I have not been able to relate Mehr's little story even. And even while telling her story, I have not been able to put it in writing properly. I have not seen that country. I have not had a serious, focused introduction to the armed struggle of that country. I have only stood beside a lighthouse on the shore of a boundless ocean to see its vast agitation at night. I have not been able to capture even the rhythm of those tides in my language. I have only described what I have seen by the brightness of the lighthouse.

That lighthouse was Mehr.

In the back seat, Bagaitkar sat with Mehr's new Dadajan, Najma's husband. Mehr had not spoken yet. She remained quiet.

There was certainly every reason for her to remain silent. This last wound was enough to uproot her entire life, her entire being. It would not be easy to bring Habib back from the jaws of Death.

Savitri and Beulah could do it. But life and death in those tales were not part of the real world. They were myths, legends. We did not have those magical powers. Probably even Mehr understood this.

Even as we progressed on the winding road to Gauhati, I felt that Mehr was not with us. What was she thinking?

When the silence became too much for me, I said, 'Habib will have to be hospitalized for a long time. You will have to be with him. You can stay with us if you like.'

Calmly, Mehr answered, 'I shall leave Habib at the hospital and return.'

I was surprised. I asked, 'Why?'

'I shall come back to nurse the wounded. What shall I do sitting there?' she asked.

'But Habib will be there,' I said.

'Habib will not be happy either if I just sat around in Gauhati. I know . . .' She broke off.

'What do you know?'

'Habib will not live. And even if he does, he will be blind.'

I did not say anything. What she was saying was true. She had understood everything now.

Mehr remained silent for a long time. Finally, she said, 'I cannot think of anything else at this point besides fighting. It's better to die fighting. I cannot even rely on Allah now.'

At this, Najma's husband could no longer remain silent. 'What are you saying, Mehr?' he asked. 'If you cannot put your faith in Allah, who will you rely on?'

'On myself.'

The old man did not say anything. I heard the echo of Amina's words in her reply. It was only when one relied on oneself that one could get a husband, a country, Allah. After having lost everything, Mehr was now looking within herself. I noticed that Mehr was not agitated. She seemed to have finally found herself.

I was proud of her.

Acknowledgements

Translating this book has been a very moving experience for me because the events that form the background to this story are a part of recent history, whose reverberations and consequences are being felt, strongly, even today in the region in which I live. Transferring this book to another language, English, presented many challenges, not least of which was the fact that it incorporates several tongues within it, seamlessly. The narration is in Assamese, but there are several portions where Bangla songs and references are brought in, along with Urdu and Hindi. Besides, there is a strong element of religion in it, of Islam, and I needed some advice on those parts.
I am very grateful to

- The Dr Birendra Kumar Bhattacharyya Memorial Trust for giving me the book, *Kobor Aru Phool*, to translate, and also for not interfering at all during the year in which it took me to complete the work.
- Dr Swabera Islam for being my go-to person when I needed advice on certain portions where the Holy Quran is quoted, and on other Islamic references.
- Mosfica Islam who also helped me with certain concepts, words and phrases.

- Manoj Deb for his help with Bangla words and songs, and also for the loan of his Bangla-English dictionaries!
- Paoli Dam who also helped out with the meanings of some of the words in the Bangla songs.
- Rezaul Islam, whose extensive knowledge of the geography, culture as well as the topographical details of Bangladesh comes from his many travels in that land, and whose memory of the details of the Bangladesh War remains sharp.
- My editor, Pranav Singh, who has done such a thorough and painstaking job of going through my manuscript, and has had a sensitive insight of my use of the language.
- Preeti Gill, my friend and agent, who is, actually, so very much more.
- And of course my publishers, especially Tultul Niyogi and Nirmal Da (Nirmal Kanti Bhattacharjee) who have been so understanding and efficient through the whole process.

Mitra Phukan,
Guwahati
June, 2016.